FINDING TRUST

FINDING SERIES #2

SLOANE KENNEDY

CONTENTS

Cover Images: © ysbrand © cookelma

Cover Design: © Jay Aheer, Simply Defined Art

ISBN-13:
978-1541061958

ISBN-10:
1541061950

FINDING TRUST

Sloane Kennedy

ACKNOWLEDGMENTS

A big thank you to Stephanie and Samantha for being such amazing Beta Readers!

SERIES READING ORDER

All of my series cross over with one another so I've provided a couple of recommended reading orders for you. If you want to start with the Protectors books, use the first list. If you want to follow the books according to timing, use the second list. Note that you can skip any of the books (including M/F) as each was written to be a standalone story.

Note that some books may not be readily available on all retail sites

Recommended Reading Order (Use this list if you want to start with "The Protectors" series)
1. Absolution (m/m/m) (The Protectors, #1)
2. Salvation (m/m) (The Protectors, #2)
3. Retribution (m/m) (The Protectors, #3)
4. Gabriel's Rule (m/f) (The Escort Series, #1)
5. Shane's Fall (m/f) (The Escort Series, #2)
6. Logan's Need (m/m) (The Escort Series, #3)
7. Finding Home (m/m/m) (Finding Series, #1)
8. Finding Trust (m/m) (Finding Series, #2)

9. Loving Vin (m/f) (Barretti Security Series, #1)
10. Redeeming Rafe (m/m) (Barretti Security Series, #2)
11. Saving Ren (m/m/m) (Barretti Security Series, #3)
12. Freeing Zane (m/m) (Barretti Security Series, #4)
13. Finding Peace (m/m) (Finding Series, #3)
14. Finding Forgiveness (m/m) (Finding Series, #4)
15. Forsaken (m/m) (The Protectors, #4)
16. Vengeance (m/m/m) (The Protectors, #5)
17. A Protectors Family Christmas (The Protectors, #5.5)
18. Atonement (m/m) (The Protectors, #6)
19. Revelation (m/m) (The Protectors, #7)
20. Redemption (m/m) (The Protectors, #8)
21. Finding Hope (m/m/m) (Finding Series, #5)
22. Defiance (m/m) (The Protectors #9)

Recommended Reading Order *(Use this list if you want to follow according to timing)*
1. Gabriel's Rule (m/f) (The Escort Series, #1)
2. Shane's Fall (m/f) (The Escort Series, #2)
3. Logan's Need (m/m) (The Escort Series, #3)
4. Finding Home (m/m/m) (Finding Series, #1)
5. Finding Trust (m/m) (Finding Series, #2)
6. Loving Vin (m/f) (Barretti Security Series, #1)
7. Redeeming Rafe (m/m) (Barretti Security Series, #2)
8. Saving Ren (m/m/m) (Barretti Security Series, #3)
9. Freeing Zane (m/m) (Barretti Security Series, #4)
10. Finding Peace (m/m) (Finding Series, #3)
11. Finding Forgiveness (m/m) (Finding Series, #4)
12. Absolution (m/m/m) (The Protectors, #1)
13. Salvation (m/m) (The Protectors, #2)
14. Retribution (m/m) (The Protectors, #3)
15. Forsaken (m/m) (The Protectors, #4)
16. Vengeance (m/m/m) (The Protectors, #5)
17. A Protectors Family Christmas (The Protectors, #5.5)

SERIES CROSSOVER CHART

Protectors/Barrettis/Finding Crossover Chart

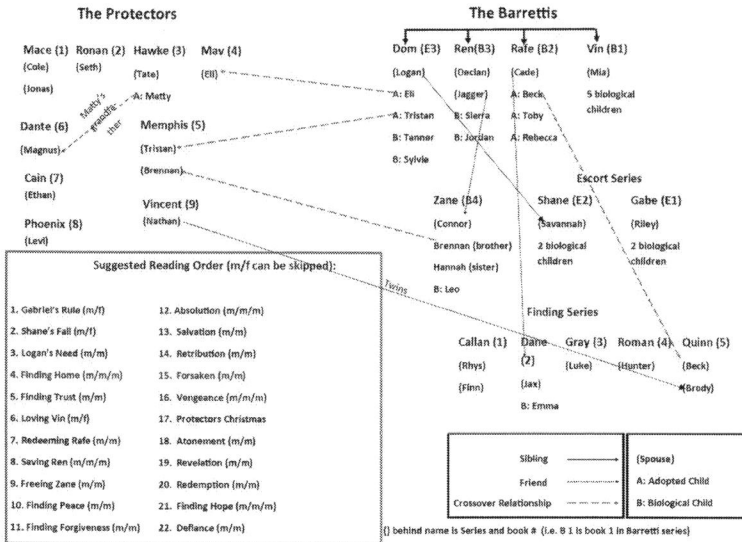

The Protectors

Mace (1) Ronan (2) Hawke (3) Mav (4)
{Cole}   {Seth}   {Tate}   {Eli}
{Jonas}   A: Matty

Dante (6)   Memphis (5)
{Magnus}   {Tristan}
                         {Brennan}
Cain (7)
{Ethan}   Vincent (9)
                         {Nathan}
Phoenix (8)
{Levi}

The Barrettis

Dom {E3}   Ren{B3}   Rafe {B2}   Vin (B1)
{Logan}   {Declan} {Cade}   {Mia}
A: Eli   {Jagger} A: Beck   5 biological
A: Tristan B: Sierra A: Toby   children
B: Tanner B: Jordan A: Rebecca
B: Sylvie

Zane {B4}
{Connor}
Brennan {brother}
Hannah {sister}
B: Leo

Escort Series

Shane {E2}   Gabe (E1)
{Savannah}   {Riley}
2 biological   2 biological
children   children

Finding Series

Callan (1)   Dane   Gray (3)   Roman {4} Quinn (5)
{Rhys}   (2)   {Luke}   {Hunter}   {Beck}
{Finn}   {Jax}   *{Brody}
             B: Emma

Matty's grandfather

Twins

Suggested Reading Order (m/f can be skipped):

1. Gabriel's Rule (m/f)	12. Absolution (m/m/m)
2. Shane's Fall (m/f)	13. Salvation (m/m)
3. Logan's Need (m/m)	14. Retribution (m/m)
4. Finding Home (m/m/m)	15. Forsaken (m/m)
5. Finding Trust (m/m)	16. Vengeance (m/m/m)
6. Loving Vin (m/f)	17. Protectors Christmas
7. Redeeming Rafe (m/m)	18. Atonement (m/m)
8. Saving Ren (m/m/m)	19. Revelation (m/m)
9. Freeing Zane (m/m)	20. Redemption (m/m)
10. Finding Peace (m/m)	21. Finding Hope (m/m/m)
11. Finding Forgiveness (m/m)	22. Defiance (m/m)

Sibling	{Spouse}
Friend	A: Adopted Child
Crossover Relationship	B: Biological Child

{} behind name is Series and book # (i.e. B 1 is book 1 in Barretti series)

CHAPTER 1

*D*ane Winters felt a large hand slam down on his back a split second after the sound of a gunshot shattered the hot air around them and then he felt himself being shoved down on top of the terrified woman he'd been treating. Panic seized him and he struggled against the heavy body covering his. *Emma.*

"Stay down, Doc!" a loud voice shouted in his ear.

"Finn!" he heard someone scream and then the sound of an engine roared to life.

Dane used every ounce of strength he had to push the man off of him, then turned to watch a scene unfolding that could have only been from one of his many nightmares. Finn, the young man he'd been giving a ride back to the CB Bar Ranch lay crumpled in the dirt, a bright red bloom of blood soaking through the front of his shirt. And just beyond him where Dane's SUV should have sat there was nothing but empty space.

"Emma!" he shouted as he climbed to his feet and located the car as it was being turned around so whoever had shot Finn and stolen it could get back on the dirt road leading away from the ranch. And they had his daughter.

"Emma!" he screamed again.

The car kicked up mounds of dust as the SUV turned sharply and raced past them. Callan Bale, the ranch foreman, tried to grab the driver's side door handle as the vehicle flew by but he bounced off the SUV and hit the ground hard. Dane managed to take two steps before that same hand from before clamped down on his arm, the heavy fingers biting into his skin.

"Stay back!" the man said to him in a cold, calm voice as he grabbed one of the guns from the shoulder holster he was wearing and handed it to one of Callan's lovers, Rhys Tellar. The man smoothly pulled the second gun out and raised it right at the SUV.

"Back tires," he murmured to Rhys who had also taken aim.

"No!" Dane shouted, his fear for his child front and center. He grabbed for the man's arm but was too late because two shots cracked the air and he watched in horror as the back tires of his truck blew out. His scream died in his throat as the truck swerved violently as the driver hit the brakes. The man next to him ripped free of the hold Dane didn't even realize he still had on his arm and began running as the SUV coasted to a stop in the pasture next to the driveway.

Fear held him immobile as he watched the stranger aim into the driver's side window and fire twice. His heart told him to move – to get to his daughter. But his mind was already trying to protect him from his loss and began shutting down. Without Emma there was nothing left. No need to eat or sleep or breathe anymore. He'd failed her, himself. It had all been for nothing.

"Clear!" someone shouted, followed by someone else yelling the same thing.

"Dane!"

Dane managed to turn his head to see Callan sprawled over Finn. Callan's desperation registered, but Dane couldn't move.

"She's good!"

His head snapped back around to stare at the SUV and Dane felt like he'd left his body as he watched the man quickly open the back passenger side door – the man who'd just fired two fucking bullets into his truck while his six-month old daughter was inside. "She's safe!" the guy yelled.

2

The words slowly penetrated Dane's mind and his breath came out in a rush. And then he heard it. His daughter was crying. Screaming actually. It was the best thing he'd ever heard in his life. And it was enough to get him moving. He needed nothing more in that moment than to get to his child but the young man bleeding out into the dirt needed him more so he ran across the driveway and dropped down next to Finn.

"Get his shirt open!" he ordered Callan as he began checking Finn's vitals. He automatically called off his findings as he worked. "Finn, can you hear me?" he said as he began working Finn's shirt off his shoulders in an attempt to find the source of the bleeding. By now Rhys had joined Callan as they leaned over their lover but Dane forced himself to ignore the pain and fear he heard in their voices. Relief went through him when he finally found the bullet hole just under Finn's collarbone.

"Help me lift him," he said as he reached for Finn's shoulders. Two sets of hands joined his in easing Finn forward. Pushing the shirt down until he found the exit wound he was hoping for, he glanced up at Rhys and Callan. "Through and through, that's good," he said, hoping the news would reassure the men. There was too much blood though and he knew if he didn't act fast, Finn would be in real trouble.

He glanced up and searched out the stranger and saw him pulling a still screaming Emma from her car seat, his big hands dwarfing her tiny, upset body. The joy he felt at seeing her was so overwhelming that it was hard to stay upright.

Callan's aunt appeared behind them and had to yell to be heard over the roaring flames that were still consuming the barn on the other side of the driveway. He was glad to hear she'd called for help because Finn would need it.

"Cal?"

Dane felt Finn shift beneath his touch and then the younger man's eyes fluttered open. They drew closed instantly and both his lovers began pleading with him to reopen them.

Dane's eyes again searched out Emma and saw that she had

quieted in the man's arms. It registered that he seemed to be talking to her and gently bouncing her even as he kept his gun trained on the cowering man at his feet.

"Coming home...saw smoke," he heard Finn say and then suddenly the injured man was trying to get to his feet and yelling Emma's name.

"She's safe," Dane quickly said, hoping to calm the young man.

"I'm sorry Dane. I didn't see them. I tried to get to her!" he explained frantically as Callan and Rhys both gently pinned him so he wouldn't cause more injury to himself.

Dane put a hand on Finn's shoulder to steady him and said, "It's okay, Finn. She's okay." He grabbed some gauze from his black medical bag and pressed it on the bullet wound. "Hold that there," he said to Callan as he pulled out the rest of the supplies he would need to stem the blood flowing from the injury.

As he worked, he tuned out the sound of the fire burning behind him and the lovers murmuring to each other and focused on the sound of the deep voice talking to his daughter. He could only catch a few words here and there, but every time he glanced up he could see that his daughter was mesmerized by the stranger and her chubby fingers kept reaching for his face.

Each quick look between bandaging Finn's wound gave him a little bit more information about the man. An inch or two taller than Dane's own 6 feet, thick black hair that looked like it needed a trim, a day's worth of stubble covering his firm, wide jaw. If the guns didn't confirm how out of place he was on a remote ranch in Dare, Montana, his black slacks, crisp white shirt and platinum watch did the job for sure. Dane tried not to notice how well the pants hugged his firm ass or the muscles that bunched under his shirt. The smattering of dark hair on the forearm clutching his baby absolutely did not turn Dane on.

The sound of sirens grew louder as the first fire truck rolled up, an ambulance right behind it. Dane finished securing the bandage as paramedics rushed to their side and he quickly rattled off Finn's vitals and explained the nature of the injury. He stepped back and wiped his hands on his pants as he went to check on Wendy, the young woman he'd initially started treating when the shooting had happened. She was still dazed from the head injury, but seemed to be okay otherwise. Callan had managed to get her out of the burning barn before she'd gotten burned or inhaled too much smoke.

He left her with a second set of paramedics that rolled up, then went to the firetruck and found a small leak in one of the firehoses where it met the truck. He scrubbed his hands clean as best he could, then went in search of his daughter. The man was still holding her as State police arrived and arrested the man on the ground. Another officer was examining the dead man in the driver's seat.

"Dane," Callan called from behind him. Dane kept moving, his need to touch his daughter overriding everything else. "Thank you," the other man said as he fell in step next to Dane as he reached the stranger.

"Look who's here, darling," the man drawled as he turned Emma so she could see Dane approach. Relief shot through every nerve ending as she smiled at him and reached out her arms. He hugged her against his chest, taking in a deep breath of her as his hand stroked over her back. His eyes drifted up to see the man's smug smile and all the relief he felt was replaced with fury.

"Can you hold her a second?" he asked Callan as he handed Emma to the other man before he could even respond. The second his hands were free, Dane swung around and punched the other man hard, knocking him to the ground.

"What the hell are you so proud of, you fucking asshole?" he snarled as the man touched his jaw and his eyes darkened. "You shot a gun into a car with my daughter in it! If those bullets had ricocheted..."

Dane couldn't even finish the thought because the image was too disturbing. The man climbed gracefully to his feet and got right in Dane's face.

"I'm giving you that one, Doc, because you don't know me," he said calmly as his hand came up and he pushed his jaw as if testing the damage. "Do it again and I don't care if your kid is watching, I'll lay you out. A bullet doesn't ricochet when you bury it deep enough inside a guy's skull that it'll take the ME a week to fish it out."

"You fired twice."

"ME's gonna be fishing for a while," he said coldly. His eye suddenly dropped down to Dane's lips and Dane felt a rush of heat go through him. *What the fuck?*

"Jaxon-" Callan began in warning.

"It's Jax," the man responded, his eyes still on Dane's mouth. He finally raised his gaze and said, "Think what you want, Doc. But you and I both know those fuckers wouldn't have thought twice about throwing your kid into a ditch somewhere if they'd gotten away...or worse."

Dane took Emma back from Callan as Jax holstered the gun Dane hadn't even realized he was still holding. The man gave him one last cold look, then turned and went to talk to the cops who were mulling around the crime scene that used to be his SUV.

～

Jaxon Reid ignored the ache in his jaw as he went to the trunk of his car and began reloading his guns. The doctor packed one hell of a punch though he supposed that any man faced with the prospect of losing his child wouldn't react much different. He couldn't even remember the last time someone had taken a swing at him and had actually gotten him on the ground. It was his own fault for being more focused on the guy's full lips than the fury in his dark brown eyes. Not to mention the kid.

God, what a sweetheart. He'd never been much for babies but when that little girl had looked up at him with her watery blue eyes as he plucked her from her car seat, a little piece of him had melted. She'd been screaming bloody murder but had settled with a few soft words and then watched him in mute fascination as he explained what was going to happen to the scumbag who'd dared to steal her away from her father. Shit, Doc would have had a coronary if he'd heard just a fraction of the things he'd said to little Emma.

Heat burned his back as he marveled at how two hours ago he'd been standing in nearly this exact spot telling Rhys Tellar that he was a free man. And now a man was dead and he was stuck in this place until he gave his official statement to the local sheriff tomorrow. On top of it all, he was sporting a sore jaw and a burgeoning erection – all courtesy of the down home, country doctor with the stick up his ass.

"Mr. Reid?"

Jax swung around, ignoring the tightening in his gut at the sound of that husky, deep voice. The good doctor stood just behind him, his kid in her car seat in one hand, a diaper bag strung over his shoulder, and a strange looking piece of plastic in the other hand. And from the expression on his face, it was clear the man really didn't want to be talking to him. Jax shoved the last bullet into the chamber of his gun and holstered the weapon before leaning back against his car.

"I was wondering if you could give us a ride home," the man managed to get out as he cast a look over his shoulder at his SUV being towed down the driveway. "It's not far, but it's too hot for Emma..." the man trailed off. Jax had no doubt that if the guy was by himself, he wouldn't have reduced himself to asking for a favor.

Jax crossed his arms and enjoyed the sight of the other man actually fidgeting. He guessed the guy to be in his late thirties. Broad shoulders, round ass – it was all working for him. He might not have been as cut as the men Jax usually favored, but his cock didn't seem to mind and he actually needed to turn back to the car and pretend to rearrange things in his trunk while he got control of himself. His slacks weren't cutting it when it came to hiding the desire that was suddenly coursing through him again.

"Callan is out looking for the rest of the horses and Rhys went with Finn to the hospital," the doctor said lamely.

"Get in, Doc," Jax said stiffly.

"It's Dane," came the quiet reply and he could hear the weariness in the other man's voice. A shard of pity went through him, but he pushed it back and slammed the trunk shut.

Dane went around to the passenger side of the car and opened the back door and began fiddling with the seat. He realized the man was installing the base for Emma's car seat. A snort went through him. Never in his wildest dreams would he have imagined his luxury car being turned into a glorified mommy mobile.

He dropped into the seat and got the car going and turned the air conditioning on full blast. It took several minutes for Dane to get the base secured and Emma settled. By the time he was sliding in the passenger seat, Jax was enjoying the first blast of cold air snaking over his heated skin. He got the car in gear and started down the dirt road that led to the main highway. A glance in his rearview mirror showed that Emma was out cold.

"Tough day for her," he mused as he glanced at Dane. God, even now the man was stiff as a board. "Tough day all around, I suppose," he corrected as he leaned back in his seat and enjoyed the cool feel of the ventilated, leather seats. Dane didn't respond to him or acknowledge him in any way. His initial response was to lay into the doctor about being wound so tight, but then he noticed Dane was staring out the window, the knuckles of one hand fisted against his mouth as if he was trying to hold something in.

Jax knew he should just ignore the man, get him dropped off at his house as soon as possible and get his ass to a hotel. The sooner he put this day behind him, the sooner he could wake up, give the sheriff his statement and get the hell out of this hotter than Hades little town.

So he had no idea what had gotten into him when he said, "Hey, she's okay, Doc" and reached out to brush his fingers over Dane's left hand. Dane closed his eyes and leaned his head back against the headrest.

"It was just supposed to be a fucking ride," he said softly. Jax felt a punch in his gut when Dane's tortured gaze landed on him. "I shouldn't have left her in the car."

"She's here, Doc. She's fine."

"Don't call me that," he said in a clipped tone.

"Look, Dane, I don't know shit about you, but even I can tell you love that kid more than anything. There was no way you could have known what would happen."

"That's just it. I'm supposed to know. I'm her father."

Jax laughed softly. "Unless you have some plan to get yourself a crystal ball, I wouldn't pin all your hopes on that thought. Sometimes you're just gonna fuck up." Dane didn't respond and Jax felt himself weirdly missing the sound of the man's voice. "So Finn is with Callan and Rhys?"

"Yeah, I guess," Dane said with a smile. "They had some kind of a falling out and he was staying with me 'till he figured out what to do next. Callan showed up at my place a few days ago and told Finn he loved him and Rhys both and wanted him to come home."

"And just when I was thinking this little town would be boring. A ménage – I bet they're gonna be the talk of the town."

A dark expression came over Dane. "Be fine if talking was all they did."

"What do you mean?" Jax asked.

Dane looked over at him. "Didn't the sheriff tell you who those men were?"

Jax tensed. "No, he was in a hurry to get to the hospital. Why? Who were they?"

"Up until a couple of days ago they were both deputies working for Sheriff Granger."

Jax remembered Emma the instant before he was about to slam on the brakes and carefully slowed the car to a stop instead. They had just reached the end of the driveway so he put the car in park. Cops? He had killed a cop? "Explain," he managed to bite out.

Dane glanced back at Emma, presumably to make sure she was still asleep. "Finn's been out for a couple years now. Not an easy thing to do in a bible-loving, rural community in the middle of nowhere."

"But Callan-" Jax interrupted.

"Was in the closet until three days ago. Rhys has been up front about it, but he's only been here a couple of weeks."

"So it was just Finn?"

Dane nodded and a pang of pity went through Jax.

"The town's been giving him shit ever since. Refusing him service, calling him names. They went after Callan's ranch too because he refused to get rid of Finn. Charged him more for things, the price of his cattle fell, cut fences, things like that. Then someone poisoned his cattle's main water supply and he lost half his herd."

"The deputies?"

"They had a run in with Callan and Rhys a few days ago. Callan said they all but admitted to the vandalism and poisoning. Cost them their jobs. Barn was payback, I guess."

Jax tightened his hand on the gearshift. "Wish I'd known that before I shot the bastard. He got off easy."

Dane suddenly stiffened and Jax saw him both physically and emotionally retreat. He sighed and put the car in gear. The stick was back up the man's ass. It was just as well since sniffing after a straight, very married guy wasn't really his thing. And if the combination of a platinum wedding band on Dane's left hand and infant daughter was anything to go by, the man was a lot of both.

No more words were spoken other than Dane telling him where to turn. The man's house was a complete surprise and Jax couldn't help but marvel at the sight of the pretty little gray, Victorian style home sitting in a clearing surrounded by huge pine trees. There was a small building behind the house and on the other side of the driveway stood what was left of a partially torn down barn. A small pasture sat beyond the barn and Jax didn't see a neighboring house or farm anywhere in sight.

"Nice place, Doc," he said as he pulled the car to a stop by the side entrance, enjoying the frown he received for the use of the dreaded nickname. Emma began to cry as soon as the car stopped moving and Dane got out and got the car seat out.

Jax opened the door and got out just in time to hear Dane say, "Thanks for the ride. I've gotta get her changed. If you want to leave the car seat base on the porch, you can head out." And just like that, Jax was dismissed. Annoyance flashed through him but what had he expected? The guy's punch had made it pretty clear what he thought of Jax's intervention in his daughter's would-be abduction.

Jax went around the car and began working the base free. It took him several minutes to figure out how to get the thing loose and by the time he was done, he was sweating again. He climbed up the porch stairs and walked into the house. The side door led into the kitchen and he set the base on the old farm style table. Boxes were piled up in corners and the counters looked completely bare except for a coffee machine and a sink full of dishes. The bright yellow paint that covered the outdated cabinets was probably supposed to be sunny and welcoming, but instead it was hard on the eyes. Maybe if the walls weren't a shade of puke green…

Emma's screaming grew closer as Dane entered the kitchen and he stopped in surprise when he saw Jax.

"Don't worry Doc, I just came in to wash my hands and use your bathroom. Then I'll be out of your hair."

The man didn't seem all that comforted by Jax's reassurances. He thought he heard Dane mumble something about it being fine but between the man keeping his distance and Emma shrieking her head off, he wasn't so sure.

Dane went to the fridge and pulled out a bottle for Emma who stopped screaming the second the tip touched her lips and began sucking fervently as her tiny hands grasped the bottle as if it would be ripped away from her at any second. Jax washed his hands, then turned to ask Dane where the bathroom was. He stopped when he saw Dane studying a stack of papers on a small desk on the far side of the kitchen.

"What is it?" Jax asked him, recognizing the tension that had entered the other man's body.

Dane glanced at him, then returned his gaze back to the papers. "They're out of order."

"What do you mean?"

"I left the bills in the order I needed to pay them in. The cell phone bill was on top," he said as he used his cheek to hold Emma's bottle in place while he searched through the pile with his other hand. "It's gone."

"Maybe your wife moved it," Jax said.

"I'm not married," came the distracted response. At any other point, the admission that he wasn't married would have had Jax asking a slew of other questions, but the hair on the back of his neck went up and he automatically pulled one of his guns from the holster.

"What are you doing?" Dane asked in concern as his eyes fell on the gun.

Jax grabbed his other gun and closed the distance between them. He shoved the gun into Dane's free hand, forcing him to hold onto it when the other man immediately tried to put it down. "Stay here," he ordered.

"Jax," he began.

"Safety's off so keep it pointed at the ground unless you hear or see anything. I'll call out when I'm coming back in."

"Jax, I'm sure it's nothing-"

"You really want to take that chance after what went down today?"

Dane paled and shook his head as his fingers finally tightened on the butt of the gun.

"Keys are in the car. Things go bad, you get Emma out of here, you hear?"

Dane nodded and Jax gave him a reassuring squeeze before leaving the kitchen and beginning his sweep of the house.

CHAPTER 2

*D*ane retreated until his back hit the counter, his eyes on the doorway that Jax had disappeared through nearly two minutes ago. The gun felt foreign in his hand and he kept his finger away from the trigger, afraid that his jittering would accidentally cause the gun to go off. Between the events of the day and the fear that was burning through him at the possibility that someone had been in his house, he was at the end of his rope. He clutched Emma closer to him and was glad when she stayed quiet and kept sucking on her bottle.

"Coming in," he heard Jax call just before he entered the kitchen. Dane tried to push away the relief that flooded through him at the sight of the other man. He tried to convince himself it was because Jax returning meant there was no one else in the house, but that thought flew out the window when Jax removed the gun from his shaky hand, his brief touch singeing Dane's fingers. God, he absolutely could not be attracted to this man. He was blunt, cocky and dangerous and the exact opposite of what Dane was looking for. Not that he was actually looking for anything at this point in his life. He wasn't even sure if the man was gay.

"It's all clear, but I want you to walk through the house with me and tell me if anything looks out of place or disturbed in any way."

Dane nodded numbly as he followed Jax out of the kitchen. They went room by room but Dane didn't see anything unusual. By the time they reached his bedroom, Emma had finished her bottle and was out cold in his arms which were turning numb from the combination of stress and fatigue.

"Anything?" Jax asked.

Dane shook his head as he sank down on the bed. "I probably just misplaced the bill. Maybe it fell between the desk and the wall or something," he said tiredly. He felt the bed sag as Jax sat next to him.

"You look dead on your feet, Doc," the other man said. "Why don't you let me take her for a bit?"

Dane shook his head. Letting go of his child was the last thing he wanted to do and having her out of his sight was out of the question.

"She can't sleep in the bed with you, right?" Jax said gently.

There was no way in hell Dane was going to try and explain how messed up he was right now so he kept his mouth shut. He was glad when Jax got off the bed and disappeared from the room. But then there was some commotion outside of the door and he was surprised to see Jax dragging Emma's crib into the room. So the guy was more observant than Dane had thought.

Jax put the crib right up next to Dane's bed but made no move to take Emma from him. "Whenever you're ready, Doc. I'll lock up," he said as he turned to go.

"Isaac used to call me that," Dane heard himself saying, though he had no clue why. To his horror, he felt tears sting his eyes. A few escaped as he closed his eyes and tightened his hold on his daughter. "It was the last thing he said as he lay dying in my arms. Love you, Doc."

Fingers brushed through his hair and then a big palm settled on his damp cheek. "Get some rest, Dane."

And then his bedroom door was closing and Dane let the tears fall.

14

"Okay baby girl, new day, better day," Dane said as he finished dressing Emma. A goofy smile spread across her tiny lips and he leaned down to blow a raspberry against her neck like she liked. She grabbed at his face and he gave her a couple more before pulling her up into his arms and heading out of her room. As exhausted as he was, mornings like this would always be his favorite. And after the hellish day yesterday, he would have even welcomed dealing with an irritable baby.

He made faces at Emma as he made his way to the kitchen and prepared a bottle. Emma bounced excitedly in his arms and let out a little gurgle as she opened to take in the nipple. Dane used his free hand to search out a coffee mug, then said a mental thank you when he saw the coffee pot already full. Not only had Jax managed to read him like a book last night during his emotional breakdown, the man had been thoughtful enough to get the coffee ready before he took off.

Dane dropped into a kitchen chair and sipped at the coffee. God, he'd actually cried in front of the other man. Dane shook his head. All the shit he'd been through since Isaac's death and he had to choose last night to get weepy and pathetic. It was just another reason to be grateful that the confounding man had left. Feeling that strong, comforting hand on his skin last night had been too tempting.

Dane closed his eyes and leaned back against the chair as Emma's sucking started to slow. The pounding in his head kept growing and he got up to search out the aspirin in the kitchen cabinet. It was then that he realized that the pounding wasn't in his head at all. It was coming from outside and his gut seized instantly at the realization of who the culprit likely was.

He quickly removed the bottle from between Emma's lax lips and settled her in her car seat. She was completely out cold by the time he had her out the door and not even the sound of a sledgehammer striking wood over and over jarred her from her sleep. Dane trotted down the stairs and came to stop when his suspicions were confirmed. Jaxon Reid was in the process of tearing down the rest of his barn. And if that wasn't enough, he was doing it shirtless.

Dane's mouth went dry at the same time that his cock stood to attention. Jax was turned away from him so Dane got a nice, long look at the numerous arcs and waves tattooed in some mysterious pattern over Jax's upper left arm, across his shoulder blade and halfway down his back. Sweat glistened over a ripped body that would put most men – himself included – to shame and tight jeans clung lovingly to a perfect ass. Dane could actually picture the muscles in each globe clenching as Jax thrust into him over and over. He chose to ignore the sight of the gun protruding from the waistband of the man's pants.

"Hey!" Dane yelled as loudly as he dared as he hurried across the driveway to the growing pile of rubble. Jax heard him and turned, the sledgehammer dangling in his hand and Dane had to force himself to keep moving at the sight of the wide chest and six pack abs that greeted him.

"Morning," Jax drawled as he reached for the shirt he had slung over a fallen beam. But instead of putting it on like Dane needed him to do, Jax used it to wipe his brow. "Didn't wake you, did I?" he asked,

"What the hell are you doing here?" Dane nearly shouted, then remembered Emma and lowered his voice. He sucked in a breath when Jax suddenly drew close to him, mere inches separating their bodies. But he just glanced at Emma, then stepped back and Dane wasn't sure if he was relieved or disappointed.

"Figured it might be better to try to get some of this down before it got too hot," Jax said as he motioned to the pile of wood.

"No! Here! What are you still doing at my house?"

Jax shrugged. "I needed a place to stay. You had a comfy looking couch. It's not, by the way."

Dane knew he must've looked completely lost because Jax said, "The couch. It's not comfortable."

"Jax-" Dane began, but then snapped his mouth shut when Jax suddenly shifted and their bodies were once again nearly touching.

"I like the way you say it," Jax murmured as he tilted his head and focused in on Dane's mouth.

"Say what?" Dane asked as a shiver snaked down his spine.

"My name," Jax responded and he leaned down and took in a deep

16

breath. God, was the man smelling him? And why the fuck did that turn him on?

"Anyone ever tell you your voice is like fine whiskey? Smooth and deep with just the right amount of heat?" Jax said softly.

Lust spiraled through Dane and he knew all he had to do was turn his head just a few inches and he'd be able to taste those firm lips. A voice in the back of his mind was trying to remind him there was something he was supposed to be saying to this man, but for the life of him he couldn't think what it was. Hot, blunt fingers brushed his waist and drew him in and Dane didn't bother fighting it. It had been too long since someone had touched him – even the months before losing Isaac had been cold and lonely.

The brief thought of Isaac was enough to bring everything back in a rush for Dane and he yanked himself free of Jax's gentle hold. He took several steps away from the intoxicating man and was relieved to feel his common sense coming back and replacing the need that had been unfurling within him. The man in front of him was just like Isaac and he'd make Dane suffer the way Isaac had, even if it wasn't his intention.

Jax watched him intensely for a moment, then sighed and reached for his shirt and tugged it on.

"You shouldn't be here," Dane heard himself stammer. So much for the sexy voice Jax accused him of having. He sounded like a whiny child.

"Look, Dane, I was worried about leaving you guys after everything that happened yesterday...last night. I also figured you might need a ride to get your car."

Dane felt like an ungrateful shit. Yeah, it seemed that for some reason Jax was attracted to him, but if that had been the man's only motive he could have done a lot with Dane's vulnerability last night, especially after Dane had all but admitted he was gay when he'd mentioned Isaac. He watched as Jax dropped the sledgehammer and moved past him, presumably to go to his car. Dane knew he would probably pay for it later, but he grabbed Jax by the arm. "Don't," he said softly. "I'm sorry. I would appreciate a ride into town."

~

*J*ax forced away the desire that had flared to life the second he'd seen an infuriated Dane rushing towards him and pulled his arm free of the other man's gentle grip.

"Sure, no problem," he said woodenly. "You mind if I use your shower to get cleaned up?"

"Yeah. But would you mind giving me a hand with a patient first?" Dane asked as he motioned to the small building behind the house.

"Uh, yeah," Jax responded as he looked around the empty driveway. He kept his mouth shut as he followed Dane, assuming the guy just needed help setting up some equipment or something before his patient arrived.

The building was flooded with light when Dane flipped the switch as they entered and Jax instantly welcomed the cool air conditioning that caressed his skin. The front room wasn't much more than a large, open space with a built in reception counter. Boxes were shoved against the far wall and a couple of plastic folding chairs were sitting against another wall.

Dane must have noticed him eyeing the boxes because he said, "I'm still working on getting my practice up and running. Lucinda's in back."

Jax followed Dane down a long hallway and tried very hard not to focus on the gentle sway of the other man's ass. So much for getting his skyrocketing desire under control. He couldn't remember the last time he'd been so caught up in wanting someone like this. On the rare occasion that the other guy wasn't interested or seemed like the clingy type, Jax had no problem moving on to the next man who'd give him the quick, no strings fuck he was looking for. But something about the strong yet vulnerable Dane Winters had him on edge and the man's rejection stung.

"I have to keep her in here for now," Dane was saying as he swung open a door leading to another room. Jax wasn't sure what surprised him more – the endless row of dog runs that lined the back wall or

18

the high pitched squealing that began the instant Dane turned on the lights.

"What the hell?" he said as they came to a stop in front of the first kennel. A huge pig stood on the other side of the door, her massive snout rubbing up against the chain link. At least a dozen piglets surrounded her, their incessant mewling an exact replica of their mother's loud greeting. "What the hell kind of doctor are you?" Jax heard himself say.

Dane shrugged. "I started with a small animal practice but decided to train in large animals too in case the need ever came up."

Jax was sure his mouth was hanging open as he turned to stare at Dane. "You're a vet?" he asked, the question sounding ridiculous even to his own ears since the evidence was right in front of him.

Dane lowered Emma's car seat to the ground and began removing the pin that kept the pig from pushing the latch on the door up. "Yeah."

"But you helped Finn yesterday. And that girl."

"Blood's blood. Two legs or four doesn't really factor in when you've got someone bleeding out."

Newfound respect went through Jax as he realized how freaked out Dane must have been yesterday beyond the shit that had happened with his kid. Dane didn't seem to notice or care that Jax was still caught off guard by the revelation and carefully stepped into the run. He pushed the pig back with his legs and held the door for Jax.

"You want me to come in there?" Jax asked, dumbfounded.

"Yeah, I need you to hold her while I check her teeth. She's got an abscess."

"You've got to be fucking kidding me," Jax said.

"Hurry up before the babies get out," Dane quipped.

Jax carefully stepped into the run, his foot instantly sliding in a soft pile under the straw. Dane leaned past him to close the door and Jax would have enjoyed the feel of the man's hard body brushing his, but he was too concerned with the monstrous pig that was sniffing his legs. Jesus, did pigs bite?

"Let's get her back in the corner," Dane said as he began corralling the large animal into the far corner of the run, mindful of the countless babies dashing around. Jax followed him and cringed when he saw Dane kneel in the straw. "Just steady her," he said as he looked at Jax expectantly. Jax finally gave up and knelt next to Dane and put his hands on the pig's body.

Dane began working the pig's mouth open and the animal tried to pull away. Jax leaned against her as Dane began speaking softly to the animal, that delicious voice of his skittering over Jax's nerve endings. It took Dane just moments to examine the pig and then he was getting to his feet. "Hold her for a sec. I've got to get some antibiotics."

"You're leaving me here with her?" Jax nearly yelled as the pig began sniffing his shirt.

"I'll be gone for a minute. You'll be fine," Dane said with a chuckle as he left the run. Jax swore he heard the guy whisper something about wishing he had his phone.

"In and out, that's what this trip was supposed to be," Jax said to the pig as she leaned against him, her dank smell permeating his senses. "Nice long drive with a quick stop to drop off a few papers, then back to the city – that's it. Twenty-four hours later and a man is dead and I'm sitting in a pile of pig shit to help out the hot country vet with the cute kid," he lamented to the animal.

"You're not exactly sitting in shit, you know," Dane said as he reappeared at the kennel door and opened the latch. Jax groaned inwardly as he realized the man had overheard every word he'd said. "You do have some on your shoe, though."

Dane leaned over the pig and jabbed a needle into her. The animal didn't even flinch.

"What the hell did I need to keep holding her for?" Jax snapped. Dane just smiled at him, then held out his hand to help Jax up. Electricity shot through Jax at the contact and he was pushing Dane back against the wall of the run before he could stop himself. The grin on Dane's lips fled when Jax's cock pressed against his. Everything around them disappeared as Jax trailed his fingers down the other man's sides.

"Montana."

"Still?"

Jax sighed. "Yeah, things kind of went to shit when I got here. I'll tell you about it when I get back." Jax raised his eyes to scan his surroundings, then felt his gut tighten at the sight of Dane coming out of the garage...on foot. "It's complicated," he said into the phone.

"Usually is," the voice on the other end said.

Irritation went through Jax as he saw Dane catch sight of him and then grudgingly walked down the block towards him. He should just get in the car and drive past the fucker and get the hell out of this piece of shit town.

"How was Chicago?"

"It's done," was all he said.

"I assumed that. How are you handling it?"

Jax ignored the question and said, "I'll let you know when I'm on the road. Should be in the next hour or so." He disconnected the call and watched Dane head towards him, the other man's gaze still refusing to settle on his. A movement behind Dane caught Jax's attention.

A man dressed in black jeans and a dark T-shirt was just a few dozen steps behind Dane. Jax went instantly on alert as the guy's beady eyes scanned the area around them as if looking for someone. Something was off and Jax was moving, his hand automatically reaching behind his back in search of the comforting grip of his gun. The man behind Dane suddenly stopped as his eyes settled on Jax and then he was darting across the road towards a non-descript, idling black sedan. The car pulled quickly away from the curb and drove off and Jax cursed the sunlight that was just a bit too bright to make out the license plate of the car as it turned the corner and disappeared.

Dane reached him and shifted Emma's car seat in his hand. The plastic base was tucked under his armpit and the diaper bag was slung across his shoulder. The nice thing to do would have been to offer to take something from the man to ease his burden but Jax wasn't feeling particularly charitable at the moment. His mind was also still hung up on the possibility that someone had been following Dane and as much as it annoyed him, the worry for the other man's safety was churning in his gut.

"They had to special order the tires for my car. I guess they're a custom size that the mechanic doesn't keep in stock."

On any other day, Jax would have drawn this out just to make the guy squirm but between his pent up desire for this man and the nagging feeling that the guy following Dane hadn't just been out for a leisurely stroll had him snatching the plastic base from under Dane's arm.

"Dr. Winters?"

Both men turned at the sound of a woman's voice and Jax recognized the girl walking towards them as Wendy, the young woman that was attacked at Callan's ranch yesterday by the would-be arsonists.

"Hey, Wendy," Dane said. "How's the head?"

A wide smile spread across her pretty features as she glanced her fingers over the small bandage covering the injury. "Good. Little bit of a headache."

Her eyes turned to Jax, then back to Dane. Jax could almost hear the gears turning in her head. Dane must have seen the direction her mind was going, but before he could deny there was anything between them like he clearly wanted to do, Wendy said, "The sheriff and Mrs. Greene got some folks together to go out to the CB Bar to help with rebuilding the barn. Maybe you guys want to stop by?"

"People from this town?" Dane asked, his astonishment clear.

Shame seemed to creep over Wendy's features and Jax wondered what that was all about.

"Not everyone sees things the way people like Mayor Greene or Doc Sanders do. Or those awful deputies. But we should have stood up for Finn a long time ago when Hunter said all those terrible lies about him. I guess today is about trying to mend some fences. At least start to anyway."

Dane seemed at a loss for words so Jax said, "When are you guys heading over there?"

Wendy immediately brightened. "We're meeting at the high school in a few minutes. A couple guys went up to the lumber store in

26

Missoula this morning and they should be getting back right about now," she explained as she glanced at her watch.

"My friends and I were just stopping to see if Jimmy needed help with his stuff," she said as she motioned to the garage behind her and blushed prettily when the good looking young mechanic waved at her from the driveway where he was getting into a small pick-up truck full of tools and equipment. Wendy's sedan was parked near the curb and Jax counted at least four people in the tiny car.

"We'll be there," Jax said.

"K," Wendy said as she leaned down to give Emma a quick tickle. "See you there."

Jax finished putting the car seat base in the back seat, inwardly impressed with himself that he managed to secure the thing without Dane's help.

"What was all that stuff about Finn and Hunter? Who is that?" Jax asked as Dane settled in the passenger seat next to him.

"Hunter Greene – he's the mayor's son. He and Finn went to high school together and I guess they were caught making out at some party by Hunter's father a couple years ago. The kid told his father that Finn assaulted him so the guy wouldn't find out he was gay."

"Little shit," Jax murmured as he started the car and followed Dane's directions to the high school. "Where is he now?"

"College, I guess. Finn said he hasn't seen him since that night."

They both fell silent as they reached the parking lot which had nearly a dozen cars sitting in it, including a couple with trailers attached to them. A flatbed truck strapped with bundles of lumber was just pulling out of the lot so Jax fell in behind the last car in the caravan as it meandered its way out of town. The slow pace meant it took them twice as long to get to Callan's ranch and by the time they drove under the metal archway with the initials *CB* on it, Jax was teeming with frustration. He owed the man next to him nothing, but all he could think about was how badly he wanted to hear that smooth, rich voice tell him it was okay. That he understood that Jax had had no choice in what he'd done. That it had been the only way to get justice for the lives that had been stolen. But Jax knew there would be no such words and the sooner he accepted that, the sooner he could get his ass out of this place and back to where he belonged.

~

$\mathcal{D}$ane's stomach was churning by the time he got Emma out of the car. The place was already buzzing with activity as people started tossing the remnants of the burned out barn into the first of the two trailers. But all he could think about – all he'd been thinking about – was that Jax had set a man up to be murdered...and he'd used his body to do it. Dane had no doubt that this Rawlings guy had deserved whatever he'd had coming, but knowing Jax had been his judge, jury and executioner had left Dane reeling and conflicted. His body still wanted the man like nothing else, but his mind couldn't deal with the truth of how dangerous Jax really was.

"Doesn't look like your friends were expecting this," Jax said from behind him, his burly presence catching Dane momentarily off guard. His eyes caught Jax's and he thought he saw a flash of longing there, but then the shuttered expression was back.

Dane looked up to see Finn standing between Callan and Rhys on the porch of one of the two small cottages on the property. Rhys and Callan were watching the commotion with confusion and suspicion but Finn had a soft smile on his face. The young man looked like he was exactly where he was meant to be. A pang of envy went through Dane.

"I'm gonna go help out," he heard Jax say and then the man was disappearing into the small crowd. Dane headed up towards the trio as they made their way down to where the barn had stood. Finn's arm was in a sling and his eyes looked heavy, presumably from the pain medication he'd likely been given for his injury.

"Hey, how you feeling?" Dane asked and wasn't surprised when Finn pulled free of his lovers and gave Dane a hug.

"Pretty good," Finn said as he released Dane and carefully lowered himself down so he could be eye to eye with Emma who was flailing her arms in excitement. "Hi Emma," Finn cooed.

"Do you know what all this is about?" Callan asked as he motioned to the group of people. Dane wasn't surprised to hear the distrust in his voice.

"Think of it as baby steps, Mr. Bale," came a sharp voice from behind Dane. Harriet Greene appeared carrying a box in her arms which Rhys quickly took off her hands. "Thank you, young man," she said with a nod of her head before turning her attention back to Callan. "It's not the whole town like it should be," she commented as she glanced over her shoulder at the small group of people. "But it's a start. It's our way of asking for a second chance."

Her eyes found Finn who carefully stood to face her. One of her gnarled hands reached out to pat his cheek. "My grandson did wrong by you. We all did."

"It's okay," Finn began to say, but Mrs. Greene shook her head.

"No, no it's not. But maybe we can start to make it right." She looked at him almost lovingly, then turned her sharp gaze on Callan. "Mr. Bale, may I borrow your kitchen for a bit? I've got some lemonade to make."

Callan nodded and then his hand settled on the back of Finn's neck. "Why don't you go help Mrs. Greene get set up and then maybe lie down for a bit?"

Finn nodded solemnly, testament to how much pain he was probably still in.

"Come on, baby," Rhys said gently as he tucked Mrs. Greene's box under one arm and led Finn back to the house with the other.

"Mrs. Greene, would you mind watching over Emma for a bit so I can help out. It's too warm out here for her," Dane asked.

"Of course," she said and tucked her arm into his free one. It took only a few minutes to get Emma settled with Mrs. Greene and then he and Rhys were heading back down towards the barn.

"Couldn't help but notice you're still with our new friend there," Rhys said as he glanced at Jax who was helping to load debris. The familiar pang of want settled in Dane's gut at the sight.

"He gave me a ride last night and today since my truck is still out of commission."

29

"We were lucky as hell that he was here yesterday," Rhys said. "Things would have ended a lot differently otherwise."

Dane didn't realize he'd slowed to a stop until Rhys actually had to turn around and walk back a few steps. "You okay?" Rhys asked with concern.

Dane shook his head. "He told me about Rawlings."

Rhys stiffened. "What did he tell you exactly?"

"Enough to remind me he's unpredictable and dangerous. And after he shot that man in cold blood yesterday…"

"Wait, what?" Rhys interjected. "What are you talking about?"

"He fired into that window without giving the guy a chance to give himself up."

"Jesus, Dane, is that what you think?"

A cold feeling settled in Dane's stomach at the disbelief in Rhys' voice. Shit, had he somehow gotten this all wrong?

"Jax shot Rollins because he was aiming his gun at your daughter." Horror swept through Dane at Rhys' words and speech eluded him as Rhys continued. "That fucker was yelling at me to stay back or he'd shoot Emma. I saw the look in Rollins' eyes – no doubt in my mind he would have done it."

Dane couldn't stop the bile that rose in his throat and he leaned over and retched into the dirt. He heard Rhys asking him if he was okay, but he couldn't stop heaving even after the contents of his stomach were empty. His precious daughter had been hanging on the edge of death as he'd stood by helpless to do anything and the only reason she was still with him was because the miracle of fate had dropped Jaxon Reid into their lives at that very moment. And he'd treated the man like shit instead of getting on his hands and knees and thanking him for saving his child's life.

A large hand settled over his back and he knew instantly whose it was. The whooshing sound in his ears finally let up enough to hear Jax saying his name as he rubbed his hand in gentle circles over Dane's back.

"I'm okay," he managed to croak out as he wiped his mouth with his shirt. "It's the heat," he said and hoped to God Rhys wouldn't contradict him. "I'm just gonna go get cleaned up," he muttered as he pulled away from the hand he wanted nothing more than to lean into. He hurried back to the small house and mumbled a quick excuse to Mrs. Greene about needing to use the bathroom, then locked himself in and tried to get himself under control. He managed to run some water over his face, but the second he looked up at his reflection in the mirror all the self-disgust came back and he slammed his hand into the glass hard enough so that he no longer had to look at the worthless piece of shit staring back at him.

~

"*W*hat happened to your hand?" Jax asked as he glanced at the bandage covering Dane's palm. He'd been surprised that the vet had asked him for a ride home considering he just as easily could have gotten one from Callan or Rhys. Not that he had any intention of letting the man out of his sight just yet since he wasn't convinced that the threats to Dane were completely extinguished.

"Snagged it on a nail," Dane responded quietly. Why the hell did the man sound so broken all of a sudden? At least before he'd just been withdrawn. But now it was like the life was draining out of him. Even Emma's incessant, adorable baby babble wasn't cracking through whatever funk the man had fallen into.

"Dane, I need to ask you something," Jax said as they neared the house. He wasn't surprised when he received no response. "The people in town know you're gay, right?"

Dane only nodded.

"Do you think they'd act on it the way they did with Finn and Callan?" Dane kept staring out the window though Jax doubted his hollow eyes were actually seeing any of the scenery that flew by.

"No."

Jax bit back his irritation at the simple response and turned into Dane's driveway. He got out and went around to the passenger side to help Dane with the car seat. Emma was flapping her arms and smiling at her father, but Dane didn't seem to notice. Jax grabbed him before he could release the car seat from the base and pushed Dane against the car door. "What the hell is wrong with you?"

Dane just stared at him, his eyes blank. It actually frightened Jax and he whispered, "Talk to me, Dane" as he ran his thumb over the man's lower lip. His touch finally elicited a reaction though it wasn't the one he wanted. It was shame he saw, not desire.

"You should go, Jax. Thank you for everything," Dane said, then pushed past him and grabbed the car seat and disappeared into the house. Even from where he stood in the driveway, Jax could hear the lock engage. Fucking dismissed like he was nothing. Jax ripped the car seat base out and managed to curb the urge to hurl it at the house. Instead, he trotted up the porch stairs and dropped the base next to the door. He got back in his car and backed out of the driveway and floored it the second he put the car in drive. Two miles later he was pulling over to the side of the road.

"Fuck, fuck, fuck!" he snarled as he slammed his hands down on the steering wheel. He was done! He was fucking done with the guy! So why the hell couldn't he make himself drive any farther? He snatched up his phone and dialed.

"You cross the border yet?" came the voice on the other end.

"I'm still in Montana."

There was a sigh on the other end. "Let me guess – it's complicated."

"There's a guy-" Jax began.

"When isn't there?"

"Fuck off. It's not like that. He's got a kid." He knew the wheels in his friend's head were already turning so he quickly said, "I think the guy's in trouble. I just need to make sure before I leave."

"Okay. You need me to do anything?"

"No. Should just be another day or two," Jax responded.

"Jax," the other voice said and Jax tensed at the softness there. "Is it really just about making sure the guy and his kid are safe?"

"Yeah," Jax said, trying hard to keep the hurt out of his voice. "He thinks I'm shit." Hell, why had he gone and said that?

Another long pause on the other end of the line. "I'd tell you to let the fucker rot and just come home, but I know you won't do that so just be careful, okay?"

"Yeah," Jax said. "See you soon." He hung up, tossed his phone in the passenger seat and turned the car around and headed back to Dane's.

CHAPTER 4

*J*ax leaned against his car and waited as Rhys pulled his
pick-up truck to a stop in front of Dane's driveway.

"Hey, what's up?" Rhys asked as he rolled the window
down and looked Jax up and down. Jax knew he looked like shit.
That's what sitting up all night in a car staring at a darkened house did
to a guy.

"You here to give him a ride to town?" Jax asked.

"Yeah, he called a little while ago. Said the mechanic finished his
car." Rhys glanced at the house, then at Jax's car. "Are you heading out
or something that he didn't ask you?"

"He thinks I left last night."

"What's going on Jax?"

Jax ran his hand through his hair and debated how much to tell
Rhys. "It's just a feeling I have."

"Bullshit."

Jax bit back a smile. In another life he suspected he and Rhys
would have been great friends and probably more since the ex-cop
was exactly his type. He gave Rhys a quick rundown of the possible
intruder in Dane's house as well as the guy following the vet on the
street yesterday.

"Does he know?" Rhys asked.

"He thinks he just misplaced the bill. I didn't tell him about the guy following him. Didn't want to freak him out over something that's probably nothing."

"Yeah, well, any other town and I'd agree with you. So what's your plan?"

Jax sighed. "Thought I'd hang out for another day or two to check things out."

"Probably be easier to keep an eye on the hot vet if you were actually in the hot vet's presence when you did it," Rhys said with a chuckle.

"Fuck off, asshole. It's not about that."

"What? You got a problem with the kid or something?"

"Jesus, Rhys," Jax said in irritation then fell silent before admitting, "He's the one who has a problem with me."

Rhys tapped his fingers on the steering wheel. "Look, I probably shouldn't be telling you this, but up until yesterday, Dane thought you shot Rollins in cold blood."

Jax stiffened. Shit, if that were true then no wonder Dane kept looking at him like he was a monster. Not that it made much of a difference since his admission about his role in Rawlings' death had obliterated any respect Dane might have had for him in the first place. "Doesn't matter," he finally responded. "Don't let him know I was here, okay? I'll stay on him after you drop him at the garage and make sure he gets back here okay. Then I'll see where things are at."

"You sure?" Rhys asked.

Jax nodded. "Good luck with things, Tellar. Looks like you've found a pretty good life here." Rhys' whole face softened and Jax had no doubt the man was thinking about his lovers.

"Maybe we'll be seeing you around," Rhys said with a grin as he drove past Jax and headed down Dane's driveway.

"Not likely," Jax whispered as soon as he was sure Rhys was out of hearing range.

~

*J*ax gave Rhys a quick nod as the man drove past him in his ancient truck. Rhys had dropped Dane off a couple minutes earlier at the garage and Jax could see Dane's fixed SUV sitting in the driveway near the entrance. He had to wonder if the mechanic or crime scene guys had at least managed to get the blood and gore out of the upholstery before returning it to the vet.

Dane came out of the garage and carried Emma's car seat around to the passenger side, giving Jax an unobstructed view of Dane's gorgeous ass as he worked to get the base attached to the seat. He was too far away to see Emma's face, but he could tell she was awake by the occasional arm movement and leg kicking. Jax couldn't believe it but he actually missed the little rug rat.

A motion in his peripheral ripped Jax from his thoughts and he was reaching for his gun as the familiar black sedan from the previous day came to a screeching stop at the edge of the driveway. The same man who'd been following Dane jumped out of the passenger seat.

"Hey!" Jax shouted just as the guy reached Dane and slammed what looked like the butt of a revolver against his head, knocking Dane to his knees. Jax knew he couldn't risk firing directly at the guy with Dane and Emma in such close proximity so he raised the gun above his head and fired. The stranger who'd been about to strike Dane again looked up and then took off running and jumped into the waiting car.

"Dane?" Jax shouted as he dropped down next to Dane who was holding his hand against his forehead.

"Emma?" Dane shouted as he tried to right himself.

"She's fine. Right next to you," Jax reassured him as he helped Dane turn so he could see his daughter for himself. The baby had gone quiet with the commotion, but promptly burst into tears.

"Dane, let me see," Jax said as he gently pulled Dane's hand away from his head. A nasty gash was oozing blood from his temple.

"Dr. Winters?"

Jax instantly whipped his gun up at the sound of the strange voice, then lowered it when he recognized Jimmy, the mechanic.

"Call the sheriff!" he ordered the startled young man who ran off to do as he was told.

"What happened?" Dane asked as he lowered himself until he was sitting on the cement. His free hand automatically went to Emma's car seat and he began rocking it back and forth.

"Fucker hit you with a gun," Jax snarled as he tried to get his rage under control.

"I didn't even see anyone," Dane mumbled. "Was he trying to take my car?"

Jax figured now wasn't the time to get into details so he grunted non-committedly and began searching through the diaper bag until he found a small towel. He dropped down next to Dane and carefully pressed the cloth to his head. His heart nearly stopped when Dane's eyes met his. "What are you still doing here, Jax?"

God, he would never get tired of hearing Dane say his name. It was like the man was stroking him with his tongue every time he said it. He was saved from having to answer when he heard a siren blaring down the street. Since the police station was actually within walking distance, it was no surprise when Sheriff Granger pulled up less than a minute later.

~

$\mathcal{D}$ane nearly laughed as he leaned back against the passenger seat. It seemed like he'd spent more time in Jax's car in the last two days than out of it. And having the big, dangerous, stunning man sitting next to him once again after Dane had finally managed to get him out of his life – if not his thoughts – was some kind of colossal joke that the cosmos was playing on him.

"How many is this now?" Dane asked as he closed his eyes and tried to will the throbbing in his head to go away.

"How many is what?" Jax asked.

"How many times have you put yourself in danger for me and Emma?"

"Not really keeping count."

"At least tell me why," Dane responded. His eyes felt heavy as the painkiller the doctor at the clinic had given him kicked in. He'd been lucky not to lose consciousness or he'd be dealing with the ramifications of a concussion rather than just a killer headache. He felt the car roll to a stop and he managed to pry his eyes open long enough to see that they were already back at his house.

"We'll talk later," Jax said as he got out of the car. By the time Dane managed to get out, Jax already had Emma's car seat in one hand and her diaper bag slung over his shoulder. When he tried to reach for his daughter, Jax gave him a dark look and Dane quickly dropped his hand. Jax stepped in close to him as they made their way to the house and Dane had to admit that for once, he was glad of the man's proximity because there were a couple of wobbly moments where Dane wasn't sure if he'd be able to stay upright. Once inside the house, Jax kept him moving until they were in Dane's room.

"I need to change and feed Emma," he mumbled tiredly.

"I'll take care of it. I'll get her settled and bring you an ice pack for your head."

Dane wanted to argue but didn't have anything left in him so he dropped down on the bed and closed his eyes. What seemed like minutes later but could have been hours for all Dane knew, Jax was back and sitting on the edge of the mattress as he pressed one of Emma's ice packs against his injury.

"Where's Emma?"

"I put her in her plaything down in the living room and she fell asleep."

Dane watched Jax in silence as the man studied him and the throbbing in his head began to intensify as his body reacted to Jax like it always did. He groaned and closed his eyes, though that did nothing since he could still feel Jax's hard thigh pressed up against his hip. "I think you should probably go," Dane muttered.

There was a slight pressure on his injury and Dane popped his eyes open to see that Jax's lips were drawn tight and his entire body seemed to be consumed with rage. Jax grabbed Dane's hand and forced him to hold the ice pack himself, then stood up to go. It finally hit Dane what he'd said and how it must have sounded. He grabbed Jax's wrist before the man got out of reach.

"Shit, Jax, I didn't mean it that way," he began to say.

"Go to hell, Dane," Jax snapped as he tried to disengage from Dane's grip. Even in his anger, Jax was being gentle because Dane knew that Jax could have escaped him with little effort. Dane also knew he had to act fast before Jax walked away from him so he dragged the man's hand down to his lap and settled it on the burgeoning erection there. Jax stilled and snapped his eyes up to Dane's.

"This," Dane said as he covered the warm hand that was now gently palming his dick, "does not help this." He pointed to his head with his other hand. "And this," he said again as he tightened his hand on Jax's, "is never going to go away while you're in the same room with me." Jax watched him for so long that Dane was about to say "fuck it" and beg Jax to tighten his grip, but then the other man removed his hand, his expression unreadable.

"Get some rest," Jax said quietly as he stepped away from the bed and left the room. Dane knew he should call Jax back to make sure the guy would at least stick around long enough to keep an eye on Emma, but then he realized that he already knew the answer. Only a bastard would leave without thinking of the little girl and Jax was no bastard.

~

*J*ax cradled Emma against his chest as he carefully removed the bottle from between her slack lips. He was content to just hold her which surprised him since he'd never considered himself much of the kid type. And since the only relationships he'd been in were the kind where talking about the future consisted of deciding whose place they were going to fuck at, the idea of being a parent someday had never even crossed his mind.

But now with this baby in his arms and her confounding father upstairs, Jax was wondering if he was missing something in his life. Jax sensed he wasn't alone anymore and looked up to see Dane leaning against the doorframe of the kitchen, his wistful eyes on him and Emma.

"How you feeling?" he asked, hoping his voice didn't sound as needy as he felt. Dane had devastated him when he'd asked him once again to leave. The second the words had left Dane's mouth, Jax had been ready to pick up the phone and call Rhys so he could hand off the vet and his daughter to the ex-cop and get his ass back home, lick his wounds and get back to a life where dodging bullets was a hundred times easier than trying to figure out the fierce, unrequited attraction he felt for a man he'd known less than three days. But then Dane had touched him – had had Jax touch him. And there had been that brief moment in Dane's eyes where he was about to ask Jax for more and if Jax hadn't known from experience how much pain the other man was in, he would have been shoving his dick deep inside of Dane's welcoming heat before the man even finished asking him to do it.

"Better," Dane said quietly as he went to the cabinet and fished out some aspirin. He sat down in the chair kitty-corner from Jax and reached over to run his finger over his daughter's cheek. Jax watched in surprise when Dane drank from the glass of water Jax had filled for himself and he wondered if the man's lips had touched the same place on the glass that Jax's lips had been when he took a sip moments ago.

"It's nearly seven. You up for some dinner?" Jax asked. Dane only nodded and Jax could still see the pain lingering in his eyes. "I'll put Emma down. You want her back in your room?" he asked.

Dane shook his head. "It's a bad habit to start."

Jax chuckled. "For you or for her?"

Dane smiled and said, "Both, I guess."

"I left a bit of a mess up in her room when I was changing her earlier. Why don't you take her while I go get it cleaned up?" Jax said when he noticed the longing look in Dane's eyes. He handed the man his daughter, then went upstairs. Since Emma's room was fine, Jax went into the bathroom and searched out the supplies he would need to change Dane's bandage and then took his time making his way back downstairs. As he re-entered the kitchen, he was glad to see the old Dane focused on his daughter, not the shell of a man who'd ignored the baby after whatever had happened at the CB Bar Ranch yesterday during the barn raising.

Dane gave Emma a quick kiss before handing her back to Jax and he carefully got her upstairs and in her crib. By the time he made it back to the kitchen it looked like Dane was starting to drift off. He took up the seat next to him and closed his hand over Dane's where it rested on the table. Seemingly startled, Dane opened his eyes, then smiled sheepishly at being caught half-asleep. But when the man's gaze traveled down to where their skin touched and didn't move his hand like Jax expected him to, Jax felt his need intensify. He forced in a breath and removed his hand from Dane's and then began unpacking the dressings he'd found. He absolutely refused to believe for even a second that his fingers were actually shaking as he was doing it.

He'd just managed to get the gauze free of the paper wrapping when Dane suddenly rose from his chair and leaned over him. Jax couldn't even process what was happening at first because it seemed to be playing out in slow motion. Dane's lips hovering over his, those warm, chocolate eyes watching him, the hand closing around the back of his neck.

"Jax," Dane whispered a second before he closed his mouth over Jax's. Desire shimmered and then sparked to life as Dane kissed first his bottom lip, then his upper one. The hand on his neck was gentle at first, the fingers stroking his skin. But then something in Dane seemed to shift and his fingers moved upwards until they were buried in Jax's hair and Dane was tipping his head back. And the next kiss was anything but soft and gentle and the instant Dane slid his tongue over the seam of Jax's lips, Jax opened to him on a moan. Dane's tongue thrust into his mouth like he owned it and Jax closed his eyes at the overwhelming sensation that bombarded his body all at once.

Dane explored every inch of him before sucking Jax's tongue into his own mouth so Jax could do the same to him.

And then Dane surprised him again by swinging one leg over him and sinking down so he was sitting astride Jax on the wobbly kitchen chair. The move put their cocks in perfect alignment and Jax immediately grabbed Dane's hips as Dane began to ride him and Jax took control of the kiss.

"Yes," Dane hissed as his head lolled back when Jax dug his fingers into Dane's hips and increased the pace. Jax bit into the sensitive skin on Dane's neck before licking his way down the column of his throat. The man had way too many clothes on, but Jax didn't even have time to contemplate removing any of them because Dane was suddenly in a frenzy as he frantically rubbed against Jax's cock over and over.

"Fuck," Jax snarled as he dragged Dane's mouth down for another kiss. Both of Dane's hands tightened in his hair as Dane ripped his mouth free and panted against Jax's lips. He pressed his forehead against Jax's and pumped his hips until he was shouting out his pleasure as his orgasm ripped through him. Jax gripped Dane's upper arms hard enough that he was sure there would be bruises and gave in to the release that coursed through him as wet heat flooded his slacks. Dane collapsed against him as harsh gasps escaped him and his lower body continued to rock against Jax gently, each slide causing an aftershock to ripple through Jax's sated body.

Holy shit. Jax closed his eyes in disbelief at the realization that the man on his lap had managed to make him come harder than he ever had in his entire life and they'd been fully clothed and barely touched. He released Dane's arms and let his hands glide down until they were resting on Dane's thighs. He could tell instantly when Dane awoke from his haze of pleasure because the muscles under his palms tightened. And then Dane was scrambling off his lap, a look of horror passing over his face as he took in the wet stain on Jax's pants, then his own.

"Shit," Dane muttered. Jax steeled himself for the verbal wounding he knew would be forthcoming. "Jax, I'm sorry," Dane whispered as he backed away.

Not exactly the words Jax was expecting, but before he could respond Dane was rushing out of the kitchen and hurrying up the stairs. Jax sighed. At least the guy hadn't tried to kick him out yet again. It was something.

~

*D*ane felt shame course through him as he pulled his sticky pants and underwear off. What the hell had he done? Dane stepped into the shower and instantly began washing away the evidence that he'd just rutted shamelessly on a man he barely knew and hadn't even managed to last more than two minutes before coming in his pants like some teenage virgin. God, even when he'd been a virgin, his first performance had been better than the spectacle that had just happened in his kitchen...in a fucking chair! And to make matters worse, his dick was already hardening again as he remembered how good Jax had tasted, felt.

He'd known that kissing Jax would be a mistake but that hadn't even slowed him down when he'd gotten out of that chair and grabbed the other man. Part of him hadn't wanted to give Jax a chance to refuse him. The other part hadn't wanted to chicken out before he got that one taste he'd been craving since laying eyes on the gorgeous stranger. Dane leaned his forehead against the shower wall, careful to avoid putting pressure on his injury.

"Idiot," he whispered to himself.

Suddenly he felt a breeze behind him as the shower door was yanked open and then Jax, fully dressed, was stepping into the shower and spinning Dane around to face him.

"What exactly are you sorry for?"

"What?" Dane asked in confusion, still reeling from Jax's intrusion. Jax crowded against him until Dane's back hit the cold tile behind him.

"You said you were sorry. For what?" Jax snapped. "Are you sorry for what happened or sorry it was with me?"

Dane opened his mouth to speak but couldn't force the humiliating words out. But when Jax cursed and turned to leave, Dane grabbed his arm and pulled him back. "I'm sorry because I practically assaulted you. And I couldn't even hold out long enough to..." His voice trailed off and he dropped his eyes.

"Long enough to what?" Jax asked, his body once again pressing against Dane's.

"To touch you the way I wanted," Dane admitted, his humiliation complete. There was a moment of silence and then he felt Jax's body shift against his.

"Then do it now," Jax said and he looked up to see Jax working the buttons on his shirt free. Dane swallowed hard as the soaking wet shirt hit the shower floor with a splat. Dane tried to remind himself that not five minutes ago he'd been reprimanding himself for starting this whole thing with a kiss but the sight of Jax's perfect chest made every thought leave his brain. Well defined pecs, hard six-pack abs, muscular forearms and huge biceps. Even Isaac with his model good looks couldn't hold a candle to this man. Dane felt a flash of shame go through him at the thought of Isaac but forced it back. Isaac wasn't here and Jax was and Dane needed to touch...be touched.

"You're perfect," Dane murmured as he reached out to trail his fingers down Jax's midsection. Jax shuddered beneath his touch and Dane felt a rush of power go through him at the realization that he was responsible for it. He kept up his exploration, enjoying the feel of the hot, tight skin. Jax groaned when Dane's fingers skimmed along his lower back and disappeared under the waistband of his slacks which were now stuck to the man like a second skin. He let the tip of one finger inspect the crease at the top of Jax's ass and he wondered if Jax was exclusively a top or bottom or both.

"Yes," Jax said.

Dane looked up in surprise and wondered if he had somehow spoken his thought aloud.

"I can see it in your eyes - you're wondering if I'd let you take me. The answer is yes. Absolutely yes," Jax said before he leaned down and kissed Dane hard. Dane moaned at the onslaught of feelings that rushed through him and then Jax's hands were skimming over his shoulders and down his chest. A pang of insecurity shot through Dane and he grabbed Jax's wrists.

"What? What is it?" Jax asked.

"I-" Dane started to say but then his mouth dried up and he couldn't get the words out.

"I would never hurt you," Jax whispered as he leaned down to press a soft kiss on Dane's lips. God how Dane wanted to believe that but he wasn't the first man to make such a promise. And he wouldn't be the first to break it either.

"It's not that," Dane managed to admit. Then he bit the bullet and said, "I don't look like you."

~

It took Jax a minute to get what Dane was trying to explain to him and he was so keyed up that part of him wanted to brush away Dane's concerns as nerves so they could get to the good stuff. But when Dane looked up at him he could see the insecurity deep in the man's eyes. Jax knew he needed to tread carefully because someone had clearly done a number on Dane in the past.

"What do you mean?" he asked, allowing Dane to maintain his death grip on his wrists. Jax could actually see Dane's skin flush red with his humiliation.

"I'm forty-two, Jax. I've got gray hairs and wrinkles. I can't even remember the last time I went to a gym. I'm pale as a ghost because I wear sunscreen religiously and I think the episode downstairs proved just how little staying power I have." The words came out in such a rush that Dane actually appeared to need to catch his breath afterwards.

"Can I have my wrists back?" Jax asked.

Dane looked down at where he was still hanging on to Jax before quickly releasing him. Jax didn't miss the flare of disappointment flash through Dane. He grabbed Dane's hands and lifted them above his head and pinned them to the shower wall with one hand.

"You ready to hear what I see?" Jax asked as Dane squirmed in his hold. He didn't wait for Dane to respond as he trailed his free hand over Dane's collarbone. "I see perfect, soft skin that I want to lick every inch of." Jax continued his path of exploration down Dane's side.

"A strong, healthy body that will line up perfectly with mine when we're fucking." His hand caressed Dane's ass. "An ass that's going to take every inch of me and surround me in fire."

Dane made a harsh sound when Jax pushed between his cheeks and brushed his hole and he bit back a smile when Dane actually cried out in frustration as Jax removed his hand. But as soon as he wrapped it around Dane's cock, the man was moaning and pushing into him.

"A cock that's going to ream me until I can't do anything but lay there and take it." He gave Dane a quick stroke, then released his dick and moved his hand up to rejoin the other in pinning Dane's arms to the wall. He intertwined their fingers and said, "Hands that gave me more pleasure in the last five minutes than I've had in a really long time."

Jax brushed his lips over Dane's. "Lips that are going to be so beautiful wrapped around my cock."

Finally, he lifted his eyes to meet Dane's. "Eyes that go so dark they're nearly black when you come."

He kissed Dane once more before finally admitting, "I'm thirty-six years old, Dane, and I've never come as hard as I did downstairs and that scares the shit out of me. But what scares me more is you telling me to leave again."

Jax knew the rest was up to Dane so he released him. Dane hadn't said a word for several long moments and Jax hated the vulnerability that was snaking through his body. But when Dane pulled his head down for a searing kiss, his doubts fled and his lust came roaring back to life. He let Dane control the kiss for a few minutes and enjoyed the feel of the other man's tongue caressing his lips and exploring every surface of his mouth. Jax had never been much for foreplay or kissing, but Dane was stealing that away from him too. Jax let his hands roam Dane's body and swallowed Dane's moan when Jax pulled him tight against his erection. Fingers worked to release the button on Jax's pants along with the zipper and then a hot hand was closing around his length.

"Fuck," he snarled against Dane's neck as he pumped into Dane's grip. His fingers bit into the globes of Dane's ass and Jax wished to God he had a condom handy so that he could feel what it would be like to have Dane riding him as he pinned him up against the wall. But a tiny bit of common sense had prevailed before he'd gotten into the shower and he'd left his wallet on Dane's bed. And there was no way in hell he was going to give Dane the chance to rethink things while he went in search of it so Jax went to plan B and dropped to his knees, forcing Dane to release him.

Jax kept his grip on Dane's ass as his mouth searched out Dane's cock and licked over the head. Dane groaned and Jax looked up to see the other man watching him intently. Jax took his time exploring every inch of Dane's length before he went back to the tip and made love to it with his mouth. He alternated between swirling his tongue around it and pulling it briefly into his mouth for a quick suck. Dane's hips kept trying to punch forward but Jax kept a tight hold on Dane's ass. He heard Dane groan in frustration, but Jax wasn't about to be rushed. Who knew what the hell would happen when this was over? If this was all he would get of the vet, he was going to make it fucking memorable for both of them.

Jax pressed his tongue into the slit on the end, then ran it all round the flared head before drawing back. He made sure Dane was still watching him when he dribbled some saliva on the crown.

"Jax, please!" Dane whispered harshly as fingers grabbed him by the hair and tried to force him forward.

"What do you want, Dane?" Jax asked as he looked up. Dane's dick actually bounced against his chin as Dane squirmed against him and Jax kept his lips closed when the hard flesh rubbed over his mouth.

"I need you to suck me!"

"Like this?" Jax asked as he took the tip in his mouth again and gave it a light tug. "Or like this?" he said right before he sucked Dane down to the root, forcing his jaw to relax so he could take him in.

"Yes," Dane screamed as he began thrusting in and out of Jax's mouth. Jax drew back nearly to the tip before taking Dane in again. The grip on his hair was painful, but he loved every second of it. He released one of Dane's ass cheeks and lifted his finger to Dane's mouth.

"Open," he ordered as he released Dane's dick. Dane did as he asked instantly. "Show me how hard you want me to suck your dick," he said harshly. Dane's mouth was like a vise on his finger and Jax smiled at how fervently Dane was going to town on the digit. God, if Dane gave Jax's cock that kind of treatment, Jax would be the one lasting less than a minute.

Jax focused all his energy on driving Dane to the brink as he sucked him deep and alternated hard sucks and long drags, adding a twisting of his tongue on the sensitive flesh on every upstroke. He pulled his fingers free of Dane's mouth and pressed the soaked tip between Dane's ass and quickly found his hole. In one quick thrust he had his finger inside of Dane to the first knuckle.

"Yes, shit, yes!" Dane screamed as he rammed his cock down Jax's throat. Jax withdrew his finger and then pushed it back in until his whole finger was inside the other man's tight body. He used his free hand to wrap around his own aching cock and knew it wouldn't take more than a few strokes to catch up to Dane who was pumping into him relentlessly.

Jax timed his thrusting finger to meet Dane's rhythm and felt Dane press back harder and harder onto his digit as Dane's cock slid almost all the way out of his mouth. He managed to look up at Dane who was watching him in earnest, his beautiful eyes glazed over in a haze of lust. Jax gave up control and let Dane fuck into his mouth as hard as he wanted, but was surprised when the man suddenly slowed.

"So beautiful," Dane whispered as he slid in and out of Jax's mouth. Jax had given countless blowjobs, but he'd never given one where he actually felt like he was the one getting more pleasure out of it. The fingers in his hair loosened and cradled his head rather than holding it in place. The emotion of it all was threatening to overtake him so Jax sucked in his cheeks hard to increase the pressure on Dane's dick. He hummed and swallowed as Dane's pace once again increased and he swirled his finger inside Dane's ass until he found the spongy spot he was looking for.

"Fuck!" Dane shouted when Jax found it and then liquid heat was shooting down his throat as Dane slammed his hips forward over and over. Pleasure wrenched through his own body as his orgasm claimed him and he pulled free of Dane's ass so he could grab the back of the man's thigh for support as Dane continued to pump in and out of him. Dane finally stopped and leaned back against the wall and Jax carefully licked every last drop of come off Dane's dick before he stood and covered Dane's mouth with his. He had no idea if Dane was the type of guy who hated tasting his own spunk, but he was willing to risk it because he just wasn't quite ready to give up their connection just yet. They'd both have to get back to reality soon enough.

CHAPTER 5

*D*ane took his time getting redressed, mostly to kill time but
also because his sated body had yet to find the energy to
move any faster after Jax had given him his second mind blowing
orgasm in less than twenty minutes. After Jax had taken in every last
drop of him, they'd just kissed and touched for what seemed like
hours and it wasn't until the water began to run cold that Jax had
released him and left the shower to get dinner started. Dane didn't
give a shit about food – he just wanted more of Jax. But the real world
was calling and he needed to remember that his and Jax's couldn't be
any more different.

Grudgingly, Dane pulled on a pair of jeans and a T-shirt and
stopped by Emma's room to check on her. He'd had the baby monitor
in the bathroom but doubted he would have heard a thing since he
was so lost in Jax. Luckily his daughter was still asleep, though he was
tempted to wake her just to have her as a barrier between himself and
the sexy man waiting for him downstairs. At least with Emma in his
hands, he could keep them off of Jax long enough to explain why what
they'd done couldn't happen again. But Dane had learned early on
never to wake his daughter before she was ready so he closed the door
and headed downstairs.

Dane found Jax standing over the stove. His wet slacks had been replaced with a pair of jeans and a black T-shirt stretched over his bulging biceps and hugged his rugged frame. He could see a little bit of the tattoo sneaking out from under the sleeve of his shirt and Dane realized he hadn't had the opportunity to explore all the curves and edges of the intricate design like he'd wanted. In fact, he hadn't gotten to touch Jax nearly as much as he'd planned to.

"How do you like your steak?" Jax asked as he began seasoning the two huge steaks in front of him.

"Medium," Dane said, his voice sticking in his throat for a second.

"I'm gonna get these going on the grill." Jax disappeared with the meat out the back door where Dane kept a small gas grill. Dane used the time to try and get a grip on himself. He put the baby monitor on the kitchen table, then searched out two beers from the fridge. He'd never been much of a drinker but he actually wished he had some of the harder stuff because trying to get through this conversation with Jax was already grating on his nerves. Jax was back within a couple of minutes and Dane's anxiety notched up another level.

"Let me take a look at your head," Jax said as he motioned for Dane to sit. The dressings that Jax had abandoned after Dane had kissed him sat untouched on the table. Dane sat in the same chair and he felt his insides twist when Jax dragged his own chair closer so that their knees were touching. Jax carefully peeled away the old bandage and Dane winced when gentle fingers probed the injury.

"Looks like there's still some swelling," Jax murmured, his deep voice drawing Dane's attention to the lush mouth that was just inches from his. He forced himself to remain still while Jax changed the dressing. When he was done, Dane tried to stand, but Jax grabbed his hand.

"Jax," he began.

"How did this happen?" Jax asked as he turned Dane's hand over. Dane stiffened when he realized Jax was examining the injury Dane had caused to himself when he'd slammed his hand into the bathroom mirror out at the CB Bar Ranch the day before.

"I told you it was a nail," Dane stammered.

"I didn't believe you then and I don't believe you now," Jax said simply, his hard eyes pinning Dane's. "Tell me the truth."

Dane snatched his hand away and stood. "You know, I'm not really hungry. I think I'm just going to go lay down." He turned to leave but stopped at Jax's next words.

"We can do this here or we can this in your room, Dane. But I guarantee if we do it in your room it will be after I've fucked you into that nice, soft mattress of yours."

Dane bristled at the threat but he had no doubt Jax would follow through on it. But he'd also spent most of his life being walked on by others and he wasn't about to let that happen again. It had been too heavy a price to pay.

"You think shit like that works on me, Jax? I'm not some random guy you picked up in a bar who will put up with your alpha male bull-shit in the hopes he'll get laid. I don't owe you a goddamn thing!" He managed to make it to the stairs before Jax was on him.

Jax shoved him against the wall at the base of the stairs and snarled, "Stop assuming I'm like all the other piece of shit men in your life."

At Dane's look of surprise, Jax said, "Yeah, I can tell that someone or a lot of someones did a number on you. I'm not trying to control you or bring you down." Even in his anger Jax kept his voice low, probably so he wouldn't wake Emma up since her room was right at the top of the stairs. "What do I have to do to prove you can trust me?" he asked Dane softly, his grip loosening on Dane's shoulders.

"You can start by not asking me about my hand," Dane said stub-bornly. It was unnerving how well Jax could read him and he needed to try and get back on equal footing with this man.

"And what happened upstairs was a one-time thing." Dane knew he was being an ass but he was feeling vulnerable and exposed, some-thing he'd promised himself he wouldn't feel after what had happened between him and Isaac.

"Fine," Jax said as he released him. Jax disappeared back into the kitchen and Dane heard the screen door leading out back slam closed.

Dane went into the kitchen and began pulling a couple of plates from the cabinets. Jax reappeared with the steaks and wordlessly put them on the table before going to the oven and pulling out a couple of baked potatoes. The silence continued until they were well into the meal.

"We need to talk about what happened today," Jax said. Dane looked at him sharply and Jax put his hand up. "I meant this morning at the garage."

Dane swallowed his food and put his silverware down. He studied Jax for a long moment and then finally said, "You don't think it was just an attempted carjacking, do you?"

Jax also stopped eating and leaned back in his chair. "The same guy that attacked you was following you the day before. He was behind you on the sidewalk when you left the garage to come ask me for a ride. He took off when he saw me."

A chill went through Dane. It was one thing to be the victim of a random act of violence, but to be targeted? Jesus, what if Jax hadn't been there yesterday? A stunning realization hit him as he remembered Jax asking him about the people in town knowing he was gay. "You think it was someone from town?"

"Maybe. I heard you made quite a big show of coming out at the hardware store a couple weeks ago."

Dane swallowed hard. "How did you hear about that?"

"One of the guys at the barn raising told me. He said the clerk was giving Rhys and Finn a hard time and you stepped in."

Dane nodded.

"Gutsy," Jax observed.

Dane shook his head. "It wasn't right what they'd been doing to Finn. What they were going to do to Rhys. I just wanted to even the playing field so maybe they'd start realizing things needed to change. I've never hid from being who I was and I don't plan to now, either."

He lifted his eyes to watch Jax watching him intently. The man seemed to realize what he was doing because he seemed to shake himself loose of whatever thought was going through him and said,

"Well, might be that you're on their radar now and not everyone's going to be as accepting as you hoped."

Dane hadn't even considered that when he'd spoken up. Not that it would have changed anything necessarily, though he did need to think of Emma. Looking over his shoulder wasn't appealing, but it wasn't something entirely new to him either. "I guess I'll just have to get better at keeping my eyes open."

"I wish it were that simple," Jax commented.

"What do you mean?"

"Did you ever find the phone bill that went missing?"

Dane tensed. He hadn't even given it much thought after that first night. He glanced at the desk and started to rise.

"Don't bother, I already checked behind the desk. It's not there. I checked all the drawers too as well as your desk in the study."

Dane knew that should bother him but he was too anxious to care at the moment. "They were in my house," he whispered as the ramifications set in. What if they'd been here when he and Emma had gotten home and had only taken off when they realized he wasn't alone? "Oh God," he muttered.

"I'd like to have a friend run a check on your phone to see if anyone tapped into it. Chances are they just wanted the number so they could harass you with hang up calls, but it would be good to check. After that you should probably change your number."

"What friend?" Dane asked numbly.

"Someone who works for a security firm out in Seattle. I started working there a couple months ago – they've got a lot of resources we can tap into if we need to. But let's start with the phone and see where that leads."

Dane nodded, too overwhelmed to do anything else.

"I think I should hang out with you guys for a few more days till this is cleared up. Sheriff Granger is checking with business owners in town to see if any of them saw any strangers in the past few days. I got enough of a look at the car that he can start a check on similar makes and models in the area."

"You want to stay here?" Dane asked. How the hell could he have the man he was struggling to resist even in this moment staying under the same roof?

"Look Dane, you've made it pretty clear how you feel about me and I have zero interest in pursuing someone who thinks I'm no better than the shit he scrapes off the bottom of his shoe." Jax grabbed his half-finished plate and dumped the remaining food in the garbage.

"My job is to protect people and whether you like it or not, you and Emma need me. So unless you want to risk leaving your kid without a father, you'll get over yourself and accept that this is how it has to be." Jax dropped the plate into the sink so hard, Dane was stunned it didn't shatter. "I'm going to go check the perimeter."

Dane watched him grab one of the guns from the shoulder holster that was looped over the coat hook and then he reached for Dane's keys off the key holder by the door. "Lock up behind me. I'll let myself back in." And with that he was gone.

~

Jax let himself back into the quiet house and locked the door behind him. He'd been outside for nearly an hour though it had taken him only a few minutes to check the surrounding area. He'd spent the rest of the time trying to repair the damage Dane had somehow managed to inflict on his emotions. Their encounter in the shower had been too much for him and he'd tried to use the time he spent preparing dinner to get his feelings back in order. But one look at Dane when he'd walked into the kitchen had robbed him of his resolve and touching the man, even just to check his injury, had put him right back to where he'd been when he walked out of that shower – wishing like hell he could just wrap himself around Dane while the outside world faded away. And then one comment about Dane's injured hand and everything had been undone. It was a cruel reminder that a couple of orgasms wouldn't change Dane's low opinion of him.

Jax went to the living room towards the dreaded couch but stopped when he saw Dane sitting on the bottom step of the stairs. He couldn't make out his features since there were no lights on except for the tiny night light plugged in just below the bannister.

"There's an extra room upstairs."

"Couch is fine," Jax muttered.

"I heard it's uncomfortable."

Hearing Dane's attempt at humor did nothing but piss Jax off further and he moved past the man and headed for the couch, pulling his gun free of his pants and placing it on the coffee table.

"I slammed my hand into the mirror at Callan's ranch. I did it on purpose."

Jax stiffened but didn't turn around. Dane's voice was closer so he assumed the man was just a few feet behind him now.

"None of my business," Jax responded, proud of how even his voice sounded.

"I couldn't stand the sight of myself after Rhys told me what really happened during the shooting." Dane's voice sounded broken again – like it had that day. Even now, Jax wanted to take that pain away.

"It doesn't matter, Dane. It's done."

But Dane continued like he hadn't even spoken.

"My father used to call me a pussy, among other things. But pussy was his favorite. I was small and skinny and terrible at sports and I didn't have a lot of friends. I thought maybe if I just tried harder then maybe I'd be good enough. So I did. I worked out, studied more, joined the football team. But it still wasn't enough. He said JV Varsity wasn't as good as Varsity so I made Varsity. Then Varsity wasn't as good as getting scouted by a top pick school. Being president of the student council didn't really count if the only other guy running was even more of a loser than me and graduating with honors didn't matter if I wasn't Valedictorian."

Jax clenched his fists but he forced himself to remain quiet.

"I left after I graduated but I guess the damage had already been done because no matter how many things I succeeded at, all I could see when I looked in the mirror was everything he said I was – weak, pathetic, worthless-"

"You are none of those things," Jax finally said as he turned around.

Dane had moved closer to him but he'd maneuvered himself behind an arm chair as if needing to keep a buffer zone between them.

"It kept happening with the few men who were interested in having a relationship with me and by the time things ended, I barely even recognized myself anymore. After Isaac, I swore that I wouldn't let it happen again. But that voice is still there – the one that keeps telling me I'll never be good enough and sometimes it's really hard to tune it out. Like yesterday at the ranch when I realized how badly I treated you." Dane fell silent and then finally looked up at Jax.

"The truth is you scare the hell out of me, Jax. But you're also a reminder of the man I'll never be – strong, honorable, brave, loyal, kind."

"Dane..."

"I *did* judge you for the way you handled the man who took your brother's life. But I know now that if Rollins had succeeded in taking Emma from me, I would have done anything – anything - to end his life."

Dane hung his head for a moment before saying, "I'm sorry if I made you feel like I was better than you because the exact opposite is true. You saved Emma's life. If you hadn't been there..."

Jax heard Dane choke back a sob and he automatically started moving towards the other man. But Dane's hand came up to stop him and he stepped back.

"Don't. Please." The desperation in Dane's voice kept him back. "The guest room is the one next to Emma's. I'll see you in the morning."

Jax dropped down onto the couch and buried his head in his hands. Seeing Dane so wounded was ripping him to shreds but what the hell could he do? His job, he finally reminded himself. He could do his fucking job and keep Dane safe and then get the hell out of this place that was making him question everything.

~

*J*ax smiled as Emma jumped excitedly in his arms as the big Pinto horse stuck his head over the fence and reached for the carrot he was holding out. "You think he likes it, baby girl?" he said as the carrot was tugged from his grasp.

"She's not answering you yet, is she?" Jax heard Rhys ask from behind him. The other man stopped next to him and eyed Emma with a look of trepidation while the baby stared back at him as if transfixed. "I suspect Dane's gonna have his hands full with this one," Rhys said as he motioned to the little girl. Emma instantly reached for him.

At the mention of Dane, Jax's eyes searched out the man and found him still examining one of Callan's horses in the open area next to the barn. "What's wrong with him?" he asked Rhys.

"The horse or Dane?" Rhys responded. Jax sent him a dark look and Rhys put up his hands in supplication. "Astro picked up a nail in his hoof." Rhys folded his arms over the pasture fence. "Not sure about the doc though."

"Don't call him that," Jax said quietly.

Rhys glanced at him but didn't question him on it. "Heard you guys had some trouble in town last week. You should have let me know."

"So you could do what exactly?"

Rhys shrugged. "Help keep an eye on things." He glanced back at Dane momentarily. "I'm guessing that whatever's going on between you two isn't making things easier."

"Anyone ever tell you you talk too much, Tellar?"

Rhys laughed and turned so he was leaning back against the fence. "I've heard it once or twice." The man grew serious and his green eyes pinned Jax. "Dane's proven himself to be a good friend to us, Jax. If he's in trouble, we need to know."

"So you can do what? Bring that trouble to your door too? Haven't your men suffered enough?"

At that, Rhys' eyes sought out Callan who was holding the horse that Dane was examining. The big cowboy automatically looked up and sent Rhys a smile. Even over the long distance, the love the two men shared was clear as day and Jax felt a jolt of envy go through him. What would it be like to be connected to someone in that way?

"The sheriff said there were no leads," Rhys said as he watched his lover for another long moment. He finally turned his attention back to Jax. "So what's your plan?"

Jax sighed. "Same as it's been all week. Stick by him and wait for them to make their next move." Jax could tell the answer didn't really satisfy Rhys.

Rhys rubbed his hand over the back of his neck, the nervous gesture putting Jax on alert. He doubted he was going to like what Rhys had to say next.

"I know you want to protect him, Jax. But what if you being here is doing more harm than good?"

Jax was glad he was holding Emma because he suspected if he hadn't been he'd have Rhys on the ground by now. "Just spit it out, Tellar."

"He's not the same man he was before you got here. And don't try to blame it on the fuckers stalking him because I saw it the day of the barn raising. It's like being around you is taking a little more of him each day."

"Go to hell, Rhys," Jax snapped, the truth of Rhys' words hitting too close to home. He tried to step around the man but Rhys put his hand out.

"Wait, just hear me out, please." Jax stopped his forward motion and Rhys continued. "I owe you everything, Jax. You didn't have to take that information to the district attorney to get the charges against me dismissed and you sure as hell didn't have to come all the way out here to bring me the evidence I need to clear my name. The fact that you did it anyway tells me what a good man you are. But the reality is that you're still just passing through, right?"

Rhys fell silent and shook his head. "Shit, I'm completely fucking this up." He finally sighed and softly said, "Just don't hurt him, Jax. He's already lost too much."

With that Rhys turned and walked away, leaving Jax to mull over his words as his eyes once again sought out Dane. His heart stopped when Dane looked up at him at the same moment and their gazes connected. Time stood still for a few long seconds and then Dane was turning his attention back to the horse. There'd been no look of longing or contentment like there'd been between Rhys and Callan. No, all that was in Dane's eyes was pain and Jax knew that Rhys was right – he was the cause.

CHAPTER 6

"*How* about this one? It's about ladybugs." Dane let Emma hold the thin, colorful book as he grabbed the stack of books he'd amassed from his search of the small children's section of the local bookshop. He made his way towards the checkout counter, his eyes briefly glancing at Jax where the man stood on alert by the front door. The ever present combination of need and longing went through him and he forced himself to look away.

It had been nearly two weeks since he'd been assaulted and there'd been no developments or leads in the case. And it had been two weeks of the worst kind of torture – being in the constant presence of the one man he could never touch or feel or taste again. The one man who made him wish for things he couldn't have…couldn't be.

"Here, you dropped this."

Dane was so distracted it took him several moments before he realized the deep, rich voice was directed at him. He turned to see the man behind him in line holding out the ladybug book that Emma had dropped at some point.

"Uh, thanks," he said as he maneuvered Emma in one arm, the stack of books in the other.

"Why don't I hang on to these for you till we get up to the register?" the guy suggested as he carefully took the books from Dane.

"Thanks," Dane said as he did a quick once over of the man. There was something oddly familiar about him. He was quite good looking with rugged features, dark blonde hair and hazel eyes. He looked to be about Dane's age though his build was more like Jax's.

"No problem. How old is your little girl?"

"Almost seven months."

"She's adorable. What's her name?"

"Emma. I'm Dane, by the way," he said as he reached his hand out. The guy managed to maneuver both his pile of books and Dane's into one arm so he could return the shake.

"I'm Gray."

Dane hesitated, then shook his head slightly as he finally recognized the man. "Gray Hawthorne, the writer?"

The guy looked around as if checking to see if anyone else had heard Dane talking and Dane instantly felt bad for how loud he'd said it. "Sorry," he said more quietly.

"It's okay. Just trying to keep a low profile," Gray said.

"Right," Dane said as he remembered the scandal Gray had become caught up in recently. Dane wasn't big on Hollywood gossip but even he'd seen the headlines. "What brings you to Dare?" he asked.

"Just a little R and R. I bought a cabin out here a few years ago and I finally have some time to use it."

"Well, needless to say, I'm a big fan."

Gray glanced at the ladybug book on the top of Dane's pile of books. "I see that."

Dane laughed and he was surprised by how good it felt. The line moved forward and Gray placed Dane's books on the counter. "I hope this doesn't seem too presumptuous, Mr. Hawthorne..."

"Please, call me Gray."

"Right, Gray. Would you like to come over to our place for dinner tonight?"

"Everything okay here?" Jax interrupted and Dane didn't need to turn around to hear the anger simmering in his voice.

"Jax, this is Gray. He's new in town. Gray, this is Jax. He's a friend visiting from out of town. Jax, I was just asking Gray if he wanted to join us for dinner."

Dane flinched at the coldness in Jax's eyes as he considered Gray. "Not sure that's a good idea," Jax said.

Before Dane could say anything, Gray turned his eyes back on Dane and said, "I'd love to." He pulled out his cell phone and punched in a couple of buttons. "Give me your number and I'll text you for the time and address." His eyes went back to Jax, the challenge clear. Shit, what the hell had he just stirred up?

Dane took the phone and put in his number before handing it back. The clerk rang up his purchases and he was keenly aware of the two big men sizing each other up behind him as he paid the bill. When he turned around, Jax suddenly reached for Emma. "We should get going," he snapped as he turned away.

"Sorry about that," Dane offered as Gray put his books up on the counter. "He's a bit protective."

"I don't blame him," Gray said cryptically as he gave Dane a genuine smile before reaching out his hand. "See you tonight...unless you end up needing to cancel," Gray said, his eyes flashing to where Jax was waiting impatiently by the door.

Dane shook his hand, briefly hoping he felt some kind of connection with the man he now knew was gay since Gray had come out early on in his writing career. But there was nothing and his heart sank as he realized why. "See you later."

Dane reached the door and watched as Jax put Emma in her car seat. Even as the man worked, his gaze kept looking all around them, watching for some threat. Jax finished getting Emma strapped in, then shut the door.

"Jax," Dane began to say.

"Don't, Dane. Just don't," Jax snapped as he waited for Dane to get in the passenger seat before he got behind the wheel. The ride home was made in complete silence. Even Emma seemed to sense the tension in the air because she quietly played with the toys attached to her car seat. When they arrived back at his house, Jax did the usual check of all the rooms before letting Dane and Emma inside. Dane was getting Emma unbuckled when Jax stomped past him and said, "I'm going to go work on the barn for a while."

The side door slammed shut and within a minute there was the rhythmic pounding of metal on wood. Dane pulled Emma out of the seat and cuddled her against his chest. He needed to figure something out soon because he couldn't take much more of this. It was time to let Jax go for good.

~

*J*ax hated the guy. Fucking hated him.

Gray Hawthorne was a very good looking man and from the range of conversation he and Dane had had all through dinner, he was a smart and charming one too. Jax hadn't recognized the man or his name until Dane started showing Gray a stack of books in the bookshelf in the living room. It was then that Jax realized the man was a well-known author and he remembered seeing articles about his most recent detective series being turned into a movie. There'd been some kind of scandal involving Gray and the man set to star in the film, a well-known Hollywood actor. By the look of things, whatever Gray had going on with the actor couldn't have been all that important since the guy was fawning all over Dane.

Dane laughed again at something Gray said and Jax felt his insides knot. Two fucking weeks and Dane hadn't said more than a dozen words to him. The only time they spoke was when Dane said he needed to go somewhere. He'd tried talking to Dane the morning after his admission about deliberately breaking the mirror, but the man had staunchly kept silent.

They spent their days working quietly around the property with Jax tearing down the rest of the barn and Dane working inside the building behind the house in preparation for getting his veterinary practice going. Dinner was always quick and quiet and Dane disappeared into his bedroom after putting Emma down for the night. Jax had been feeling wracked with guilt since his conversation with Rhys about him being the cause of Dane's pain, but seeing him so open and free with Gray had Jax wanting to put his hand through the nearest wall. Fearing he would do just that, Jax pushed the plate with his untouched food aside and stood up and left the kitchen. The remnants of Dane's barn were calling his name.

～

ane flinched every time he heard the sledgehammer make contact with the wood. The sun had just started falling behind the clouds on the horizon when Dane had glanced out the window to see that Jax had finished tearing the last of the barn's supporting structure down. Dane had gone up to put Emma to bed and had returned to sit in the kitchen to wait for Jax to come in. That had been forty-five minutes ago.

Dane stood up to look out the window once more. He could only see Jax's outline but there was enough light from the motion activated floodlights that Jax had installed to see that Jax was breaking down some of the bigger pieces of wood. The man had been going non-stop for nearly two hours and Dane knew he had to be hurting from the exertion. Grabbing the baby monitor, he headed outside. He had no doubt that Jax heard him coming, but the man didn't turn around or slow down.

"Jax, it's late. Come inside."

Jax continued to ignore him so Dane reached for the sledge hammer on Jax's next downward strike. His arm wrenched at the power that was still behind the force of the swing but Jax stopped the motion before Dane got seriously hurt. Jax ripped the sledge hammer from him, his chest heaving as his cold eyes latched onto Dane. A ripple of fear went through Dane at how calm the man was and he was instantly transported back to the day of the fire when Jax had shot Rollins.

"Jax," Dane started to say but snapped his mouth shut when Jax threw the sledge hammer to the ground and stalked back to the house.

"We need to talk," Dane said when he caught up to Jax inside of the kitchen where Jax was drinking down the entire contents of a bottle of water.

"You've had two weeks to talk to me, Dane. We're not going to start now just because you feel like it."

"Things need to change."

"They already have," was all Jax said as he headed for the stairs.

Dane grabbed him by the arm. "What does that mean?"

"Some guys will be here in the morning to install an alarm system. Rhys got back from Chicago this afternoon so starting tomorrow he's going to keep an eye on things and take you to town when you need to go."

Dane realized what Jax hadn't said. "You're leaving?"

Jax didn't answer. He just pulled his arm free and went up the stairs. Dane waited for that feeling of relief that was supposed to surge through him at the knowledge that he would soon be free of the torment that being around Jax brought. But it didn't come. Instead there was a crushing, physical pain in his chest and he actually had to sit down on the stairs and wait for it to pass. What the hell was wrong with him? He was getting his life back. In less than twelve hours it would be him and Emma again and they could get back to the life he'd brought them here to live. In a few short weeks he'd be in a position to open his practice. He'd have his career and his daughter. That was enough…it was supposed to be enough.

～

*J*ax had just managed to pull his boxers on after his quick shower when the door to his room was thrown open. Dane stood there, baby monitor in hand, eyes wide, almost frantic looking.

"Out," Jax said, his fury like a living thing beneath his skin. He was done letting this man tear him apart.

Instead of leaving, Dane moved into the room and closed the door. He walked past Jax and carefully put the baby monitor on the nightstand. Then his trembling fingers went to the hem of his shirt and in one quick motion it was over his head and off.

The sight of Dane's beautiful chest actually had Jax moving before he caught himself. "Get the fuck out, Dane!" Jax nearly yelled, remembering at the last minute that Emma was asleep one room over.

Dane ignored his outburst and reached for the button on his jeans. Jax was on him in three strides and grabbed his arm. He yanked him towards the door with every intention of throwing him out but Dane fought him and somehow Jax ended up pressed back against the door as Dane's hand snaked down his shorts and grabbed his erection. The feel of the warm, rough palm encircling him made Jax pause in his efforts and that was all it took for Dane to pull free and drop to his knees. It was on the tip of Jax's tongue to tell Dane no but then that lush mouth was pulling him in and sucking him down.

"Jesus," Jax whispered as gentle fingers caressed his balls while his entire cock was bathed in wet heat. He looked down to see Dane's nose pressed up against his groin and he groaned when Dane swallowed around him. Dane hung there for several long seconds before pulling back up. His eyes looked up to search out Jax's before sucking him all the way back in. Jax knew he should stop this – he should grab Dane by the hair and force him to stop because the only place this would lead would cause more pain for both of them. So he did grab Dane's hair, but instead of pulling him off, he held the other man in place as he mercilessly pushed his dick further down Dane's throat.

"Is this what you want?" he asked harshly as he fucked in and out of Dane's willing mouth. In response, Dane relaxed his jaw and caressed him with his tongue on every pass and the fingers holding his balls moved up to palm his ass. Dane gagged as Jax pushed in further and Jax waited to see if the man would finally cry uncle. But instead, Dane's grip on Jax's ass tightened and he held Jax there as Dane fought his gag reflex.

Dane's acquiescence did nothing to ease Jax's anger and he finally grabbed Dane's jaw and forced him to release his hold on his cock. Jax held him there for a long moment as he tried to force the words out that would drive Dane away once and for all. One swipe at Dane's insecurity about his looks was all it would take. Instead, Jax yanked Dane up and crushed their mouths together. The kiss was brutal, cruel even, but Dane took it all, his moans of pleasure evidence that he didn't have a problem with the rough treatment.

Jax ripped his mouth free and shoved Dane away. "You want a quick fuck, you can get it from your new boyfriend. I'm not interested."

"Your body says otherwise," Dane said as he once again reached for the button on his pants. The zipper was next and the sound had Jax's dick hardening further. Pre-come leaked from the head and he saw Dane actually lick his lips at the sight. Jax closed the distance between them and grabbed Dane by the throat.

"Do you have any idea what I'm going to do to you if this goes any further?" he whispered coldly. "No pretty words, no loving kisses. There won't be anything sweet about what will happen. And it sure as shit won't change what happens tomorrow. Is that what you want?"

"I'll take whatever part of you I can get," Dane whispered softly.

Heat slammed into Jax and he backed Dane up and then spun him around and shoved him face down onto the bed. He wasn't gentle when he yanked Dane's pants and underwear down. It took him only seconds to search out the lube in his nightstand drawer and he dribbled some onto Dane's quivering hole. He worked the lube into Dane's body with one finger, then rolled a condom down his length. Dane's body was shaking but Jax forced himself to ignore it, his anger still too raw. He put some lube on his dick and then pressed it up against Dane's ass. He leaned over the other man and said, "Last chance to stop this."

Dane remained stubbornly mute and Jax reared back and began pushing inside him. Dane groaned as his body fought the intrusion but Jax was relentless. Dane cried out as his body gave up the fight and Jax sank all the way inside of him. Jax closed his eyes in pleasure as Dane's heat engulfed him and the pressure on his cock intensified. His hands sought out Dane's hips as he pulled out nearly all the way before shoving back in to the root. Dane grunted beneath him but didn't protest. Jax slammed into him a few more times and still Dane didn't say anything. Jax's anger began to fade as he realized what Dane had said was true – he *would* take any part that Jax gave him, even if it meant there was no pleasure in it for him. Jax pulled out of Dane.

"Don't stop, Jax. Please!" Dane said as he looked over his shoulder, his pretty brown eyes full of desperation.

Jax reached down and rolled Dane onto his back and then lowered his body down onto him and kissed him. Dane instantly opened and let Jax in and Jax took his time exploring Dane's mouth before releasing him and saying, "Why are you doing this?"

Dane's hand came up to stroke over the back of Jax's neck. "I needed a little more of you before you left," he admitted before pulling Jax down for another lingering kiss.

"What about Gray?" Jax asked.

"It was just dinner, Jax. That's it."

"He made you laugh."

"You make me feel," Dane whispered.

The admission had Jax plundering Dane's mouth and he reveled in the feel of Dane's palms running along his back and down to cup his ass. He let Dane rub their cocks together before the need took over and he sat up, stripped the remaining clothes off of Dane and urged him to move towards the middle of the bed. Jax pushed Dane's legs up and apart and pressed his cock against his hole once more. He let his eyes connect with Dane's as he eased forward and when they were finally joined, Jax leaned down and kissed Dane as he slowly began thrusting in and out of him.

~

The pleasure of feeling Jax sliding gently in and out of him was so much more than Dane had expected after the rough start. He'd known that he'd pushed Jax too far and had been honest when he'd said he would take whatever he could get. He'd fully expected things to be over by now with him back in his own room nursing a sore ass after a quick, rough fuck. It still would have been better than watching Jax walk away from him tomorrow without

SLOANE KENNEDY

having known the feel of the other man deep inside his body. So he had gladly taken what Jax had offered and had ignored the discomfort that came with the minimal preparation. Jax's first thrusts had bordered on pain, but then the pleasure had begun to override the burn and he'd started to welcome the harsh pummeling. And then Jax had stopped and Dane was sure it was over – that Jax had found the perfect punishment. Drive him to the edge and leave him hanging.

Dane should have known better that even in his fury, Jax would never truly hurt him. And what they were doing now was exactly what Jax had threatened it wouldn't be – loving and sweet. Because even as Jax's rhythm increased, his kisses were gentle and soft and when he finally stopped kissing Dane's mouth it was only so that he could press kisses to Dane's neck instead. Jax's hands went under Dane's back and curled up around his shoulders so that every part of their bodies were touching as Jax powered in and out of him.

"You're so beautiful, Dane. So fucking perfect," Jax whispered in his ear. Dane wanted to cry at the pretty words Jax had also sworn wouldn't happen.

Dane felt his body begin to tingle in anticipation of what was coming and he wrapped his arms around Jax's back, wishing he could hold the end off for just a little longer.

"Come, baby," Jax whispered against his lips.

Dane shook his head, too overcome with emotion to try to explain why he wasn't ready.

"We have all night, Dane. I want you to come with me," Jax said as he thrust his tongue into Dane's mouth. Dane felt a hand close around his cock and he knew the added pressure would end him. His body drew tight as Jax kept up the unrelenting pace and then Jax shifted just enough to brush his prostate. The orgasm hit him hard and went on and on as Jax continued to strike the same spot inside him over and over. Hot liquid coated his stomach and Jax pulled free of his mouth long enough to shout his name as his cock began pulsing inside of Dane.

Jax continued to pump in and out of him as their orgasms eased and then Jax let all his weight press onto Dane. Dane felt Jax's lips trailing kisses along his collarbone and up his neck and in the instant before Jax covered his mouth with his own, Dane knew he'd made a terrible mistake in thinking that it would somehow be easier to let Jax go after this.

~

"*I*saac, no!"

"Dane, wake up!" Jax sad as Dane flailed against him.

"Isaac, please! Stay with me, Isaac. Don't close your eyes!"

"Dane!" Jax shouted as he covered Dane's body with his. Tears were streaming down Dane's face. "Baby, please, wake up for me," Jax urged as he grabbed Dane's flailing arms and held them gently on the bed. Dane's eyes suddenly flew open and he struggled in Jax's hold.

"It's me, Dane. It's Jax," he said quickly as he eased some of his weight off of Dane. Dane instantly relaxed beneath him and Jax helped him sit up so he could catch his breath. He ran his hand up and down Dane's back until the harsh breaths slowed.

"Sorry," Dane muttered as he wiped at his wet face with his hands.

"It's okay," Jax said as he continued to stroke Dane's back. "You want to talk about it?"

"Not really," Dane said.

"Do they happen a lot?" Jax asked as he eased them back down and pulled Dane onto his chest.

Dane nodded. "Most nights since the shooting," he admitted. "Before that maybe a couple times a week."

"Was Isaac your husband?" Jax asked as he gently touched the wedding band Dane continued to wear.

Another nod.

"What happened to him, Dane?"

Dane was silent for a long time, then the hand on Jax's side gripped him hard as if Dane was looking for something to keep him in the moment.

"He was murdered."

Jax forced himself to remain relaxed. He let his fingers trail through Dane's hair, adding just enough pressure to ease some of the tension in Dane's wound up body. "Tell me," he urged.

Dane sighed and then the fingers biting into his side eased. "Isaac was a lot like you. Impossibly beautiful, strong, hard-headed. I met him when I treated a K-9 officer that had been shot protecting his handler."

"Isaac was a police officer?"

Dane nodded against his chest. "SWAT actually. We hit it off right away but I was reluctant to pursue anything because he was ten years younger than me and I didn't have a very good track record when it came to relationships. But Isaac was the type of guy who got whatever he wanted and for some reason he wanted me," Dane said on a constricted laugh.

"We got married a few years ago and he started talking about having a family. He wanted lots of kids but I wasn't so sure since my childhood hadn't been that great. I guess I was afraid I might end up like my father."

Jax wanted to interject, but kept his mouth shut so that Dane would continue.

"We found a surrogate and decided to use both our sperm to fertilize the donated eggs. That way either one of us could end up being the biological father."

Dane fell silent again and Jax waited him out. The story clearly didn't have a happy ending and he suspected the in between might not be all great either.

"The surrogate miscarried twice. The stress was hard on us but we were overjoyed when the third pregnancy looked like it would go to term. But something in Isaac started to change as the due date grew closer. Maybe I did too, I don't know. We stopped talking like we used to and he spent more and more time working. I thought he was just freaking out about being a parent so I tried to let it go. But even after Emma was born he struggled with the stress of having a baby to take care of. We both did."

Dane's grip on him tightened again and Jax settled his hand on his back. "Tell me," he urged.

"About a month after Emma was born he admitted that he'd been cheating on me for months."

Jax closed his eyes as he imagined the pain and betrayal Dane must have felt.

"He didn't know exactly how many men there'd been but he swore he only loved me. I threw him out and told him I never wanted to see him again."

Jax felt Dane's tears against his skin and he wished in that instant that he hadn't made Dane do this.

"I ignored his calls for a few weeks. When I finally did talk to him I told him I was going to file for divorce but that we would share custody of Emma. He begged me to meet him at this diner we used to go to every week when we were dating and I agreed. He kept telling me how much he loved me and how sorry he was. I told him it was too late, gave him his options for being a part of Emma's life after the divorce and left. I was at my car when I heard the first gunshot."

Dane buried his face in Jax's chest as he began to cry. "He was coming after me when he heard a man screaming at his wife. Isaac tried to intervene and the man shot him in the chest. Then he shot his wife and then himself. I tried to stop the bleeding but it was too late. He told me he was sorry and then he said he loved me and then he was gone. I didn't even get a chance to forgive him!"

Jax dragged Dane further up his body and held him as the other man sobbed. "I'm sorry," he whispered against Dane's ear as he held him tight. He just kept repeating the words over and over until Dane quieted and eventually fell asleep in his arms.

～

Jax packed up the rest of his clothes and took one last look at the empty bed before leaving the room. He wasn't sure at what point Dane had left this morning but waking up alone had been a good reminder that what had happened between them had been a one-time thing and his life would finally get back to normal today. He was certain the knot of pain in his chest would ease the second he hit the highway and would be a distant memory by the time he reached Seattle.

Jax glanced in Emma's room as he passed and saw that it was empty. He'd ended up sleeping in longer than he usually did since he'd stayed awake long after Dane had finally fallen back asleep. He also suspected Dane had been extra quiet in sneaking out of his bed so there wouldn't be that awkward moment where Dane would have to tell him it had been fun and then wish him a safe journey home.

"Should we go visit Kirby today?" Jax heard Dane say. He rounded the kitchen and stopped short at the sight of Dane sitting in front of Emma's high chair. Every time he reached out to pretend to tickle his daughter, a big smile split her tiny mouth and she'd laugh before Dane even touched her. Jax leaned against the doorframe and realized it would be these moments he'd miss the most.

Dane must have sensed his presence because he glanced over his shoulder and quickly stood. Heat flooded his cheeks and Jax wasn't sure if it was because the man was embarrassed to be caught playing silly games with his daughter or because he was thinking about the things they'd done together last night.

"Morning," Dane said as he began cleaning up the breakfast he'd been feeding Emma.

"Morning." Jax glanced at his watch. "Rhys should be here soon so I'll head out once he gets here. I'm just gonna go pack up my car," he said. Packing up his car really only consisted of putting his bag in the trunk but he wasn't about to extend the awkward moment between him and Dane by waiting in the house.

"He's not coming," he heard Dane say as he opened the side door. He stilled and looked up.

"What?"

"Rhys isn't coming. I called and told him not to," Dane said, his voice slightly higher than normal.

"Why did you do that?" Jax asked in irritation. Was Dane really going to choose this moment to be stubborn? When he literally had his foot out the door?

Dane suddenly turned around and began rinsing out the dishes in the sink. "Because I don't want him here - I want you here. I know it's selfish of me to ask since you have a life to get back to, but I'm not ready to let you go yet. But if you stay, stay because you want to and not because you feel obligated-"

Jax didn't give Dane a chance to finish because he'd already been moving when Dane admitted he wasn't ready to let him go. He cut off Dane's final words when he spun him around and kissed him hard. Dane's wet hands pressed against his shirt and then wrapped around his neck as Dane kissed him back. Jax reminded himself that Emma was in the room so bending Dane over the kitchen table wasn't an option. He pressed Dane back against the sink and let their tongues duel playfully. Only the sound of the doorbell kept him from sliding his hands down to the other man's ass like he wanted.

"Alarm guys," he said against Dane's mouth when he tried to retreat but Dane refused to let him go.

Dane sighed and dropped his head to Jax's chest, then released him.

"Tonight," Jax whispered before giving Dane another hard kiss and then going to answer the door.

~

*J*ax smiled as Dane sat awkwardly on the horse as Finn led him around the arena, his arm no longer in the sling.

"Say hi to Daddy," Jax said to Emma as Dane rode past them. Dane waved at his daughter and then sent him a heated look. Jax was increasingly glad he'd decided to change into jeans before coming out to the ranch since they were somewhat more effective at hiding his seemingly ever-present erection.

"A vet who's never been on a horse before," Callan said as he appeared next to them and leaned his arms over the fence. "Wish I could say he was a natural," Callan chuckled.

Jax wanted to say that the only thing he cared about Dane riding was him but kept the thought and the images that went with it to himself. "Barn looks good," he said instead as he glanced at the nearly finished barn behind them.

"Yeah, people keep showing up every day to put the finishing touches on it." Jax wasn't surprised by the disbelief he heard in Callan's tone. He knew the ranch foreman wasn't going to be able to easily brush aside all the cruelty that had been heaped upon him and Finn.

"He doing okay?" Jax asked as his eyes fell on the younger man who was in the process of explaining something to Dane about his position on the horse.

"Pretty good. Still a few nightmares. More about her than the actual shooting," Callan said as he motioned to Emma. "You mind?" he asked as he held his hands out.

"Sure," Jax said as he handed the baby over. He wasn't surprised when Emma easily accepted Callan. "Where's Rhys?" he asked as he glanced around the property.

"He went to go check on the herd when he heard you guys were coming over." Callan turned Emma so she could watch her father. "He's feeling pretty guilty about the things he said to you."

"He told you about that, huh?"

Callan smiled. "No room for secrets in our family. There were too many of those for too long," he remarked as his eyes went to Finn. Just like with Rhys, Finn looked up as if sensing his lover's gaze and the young man smiled.

"He's got nothing to feel guilty about. He was just saying it like he saw it."

"He said you were planning on leaving today."

Jax's eyes went to Dane and he felt a well of emotion when Dane drew his attention away from Finn long enough to send Jax a warm smile. "How did things go in Chicago?"

Callan sighed but Jax was grateful when he didn't argue the change of subject. "Good. Charges were dismissed and the city is offering a really generous settlement. The press is having a field day. Even the national news has picked it up. He granted one of them an interview in the hopes things would settle down but he's worried they're going to track him down out here."

"That's a pretty good possibility," Jax said.

"Your name never came up. Not even by the FBI when they offered their apologies for not believing him about Rawlings."

Jax sighed. "Doesn't surprise me. Not like they want to admit one of their former agents went to extremes to catch the killer they let slip through their fingers."

They both fell silent as Dane rode past again. Once he was out of hearing Callan said, "He's a good man."

Jax readied himself for what he knew was coming next.

"I'm glad you two found each other."

That was it? Jax glanced at Callan who was bouncing Emma gently in his arms. When he saw Jax staring at him he said, "What?" though his tone indicated he already knew what Jax was thinking. *Smart bastard.*

"Nothing," Jax said before turning his attention back to the arena. After a moment he said, "Tell Rhys we're good."

~

"I'm gonna put her down," Dane said quietly as Jax disarmed the alarm system. He went upstairs and carefully put Emma down in her crib and let his hand rest on her back until she settled again and then he left the room, softly closing the door behind him. It was ridiculous to suddenly be this nervous around Jax considering what he'd said to the man this morning. He'd woken up still wrapped in Jax's arms and if he hadn't heard Emma stirring over the baby monitor, he would have gladly stayed where he was. He'd loved how tight Jax had held him but he'd had a hell of a time disengaging himself from Jax's strong grip without waking him up. He supposed it had been cowardly to sneak out the way he had but he was just too emotionally raw from their night together and had needed the time to build up his walls before facing Jax.

His routine with getting Emma ready for the day had been the same but he'd been tense and unfocused as he waited for Jax to come down the stairs and walk out of his life forever. The anxiety had kept building and building and Dane hadn't even realized he'd picked up his cell phone and dialed until Rhys answered. He'd given Rhys a quick order not to come and hung up before the man could even ask why and then Dane had waited and worried and doubted. And then Jax was standing there in the doorway, his black bag in hand and Dane had somehow managed to get the words out, though he'd been unable to face Jax when he did it. When Jax had kissed him mid-sentence, Dane had finally felt like a weight had been lifted from his chest and he felt the relief in every cell of his body.

Between the alarm guys installing the system and the impromptu riding lesson, he and Jax hadn't had much time to talk and the air had been awkward between them during the car ride. Dane had no idea what their relationship was or if they even had one. It seemed unlikely that Jax would stay just for the sex, even if it had been mind-blowing sex. At least for him – maybe it was just okay for Jax.

Isaac had always reassured him that what they had was great but he'd looked to someone else for something Dane apparently couldn't give him. So what the hell did he have to offer someone like Jax? What kind of future would Jax have in a hick town with one stop light and no job prospects for someone who carried guns around like they were an accessory? And what would happen when Jax got tired of him and saw him for the man he really was?

"She go down okay?"

Dane snapped his eyes up and realized he'd been so lost in thought that he'd walked down the steps without even realizing it. He glanced over his shoulder and saw that Jax was sitting on the couch, his glorious, naked chest on display. A bottle of lube and a condom sat on the coffee table. Dane's mouth went dry at the sight but he managed to choke out a "Yeah."

"Thought you might want to show me what you learned in your riding lesson today," Jax drawled as he shifted his body so his legs were slightly spread in invitation. Dane's cock went from semi-hard to downright painful almost instantly and his body was moving before his brain could even catch up. He stopped between Jax's legs.

"What's the first thing you learned?" Jax asked.

Lust slammed through Dane as he said, "How to properly prepare my mount."

Jax seemed relaxed but Dane saw a tremor go through him. "Show me," Jax ordered, his voice uneven.

Dane didn't hesitate and dropped to his knees. He let his hands glide along Jax's thighs and then brush over his cock as he reached for the button on his jeans. He managed to get it free and then pulled the zipper down slowly as he let his fingers trail over Jax's abdomen. The muscles rippled beneath his touch and Jax sucked in a breath. Dane grabbed the waistband of Jax's jeans and tugged and Jax lifted enough so he could work the pants and underwear off. Jax had been insightful enough to remove his shoes and socks so Dane had him completely naked within seconds.

Dane didn't know where the hell to start because every part of Jax was tempting him. Dane reached up and ran his fingers along Jax's chest and then down to his sides, testing every muscle as he went. He let his tongue follow the path of his fingers and felt Jax's cock pressing impatiently against him. But Dane had a lot of ground to cover and he took his time biting and licking and sucking every surface of Jax's chest and abdomen. His thighs were next and he enjoyed the feel of the rough hair on his tongue. His hands kept busy too and Jax stiffened when Dane finally used them to spread Jax's legs open wider. When Dane ignored Jax's cock in favor of his abdomen once again, Jax said his name in warning.

Dane looked up to see Jax's eyes dark with passion and his fists were clenched where they sat on the back of the couch. Dane kept his eyes on Jax as he stroked his fingers over Jax's stiff flesh. Jax hissed but didn't close his eyes. Dane teased him with a couple of brief strokes that he knew wouldn't give Jax any kind of relief and just as the frustrated man opened his mouth again – probably to curse him for the torment he was inflicting – Dane dropped his head and licked his way up from the base of Jax's cock to the tip.

"Yes," Jax moaned as his head fell back against the couch. Dane did it a few more times, relishing the strong, musky flavor that flooded over his tongue. He stopped at the crown and licked over the slit there a few times, then sucked on it gently.

"Jesus," Jax shouted as he tried to thrust into Dane's mouth. But Dane had a hold on his base and refused to take him any deeper. He kept alternating swirling his tongue around the flared head and sucking just the tip into his mouth. As Jax's moans increased, Dane took him further and further inside and then finally relaxed his jaw enough so that Jax could slide all the way down his throat. He released his hold on Jax's cock and was instantly rewarded with an upward thrust. Dane dragged his mouth up and down Jax's dick over and over, increasing the pressure each time. After several torturous drags, he let Jax's cock fall free of his mouth and made sure Jax was watching him when he stuck a finger in his mouth. He used his free hand to pull Jax's body further down the couch so his ass was hanging off the edge.

Jax was transfixed on the finger in Dane's mouth and he held his breath when Dane took the wet digit and began probing Jax's crease. He felt the wrinkly skin around Jax's opening and applied pressure. Jax groaned and lifted his legs so that his feet were braced on the edge of the couch giving Dane an unfettered view of the small hole fluttering in anticipation of his touch. Dane brushed over it a few times before changing his mind and pulling his hand away and using his tongue instead.

"Fuck, fuck, fuck!" Jax yelled as Dane licked him over and over. Dane hadn't been sure if this was something Jax would go for but the man's enthusiastic cries made it clear that it wasn't off limits like it had been with Isaac. Dane kept up his sensual torture until Jax warned him he was about to come. Dane sat back on his heels and licked his lips as Jax lowered his legs. The forbidden flavor had his own dick leaking in his jeans and he quickly stood and pulled off his clothes. Jax watched hungrily and shifted himself so he was sitting further back on the couch again.

The hold Dane had on his desire began to quickly disappear and he grabbed the lube and condom. His fingers trembled as he rolled the condom down Jax's shaft and he quickly put some lube on the latex covering. He reached around to prepare himself with a generous amount of the lube, aware of Jax's lust-filled gaze on him the whole time. Whatever game they'd been playing was over as Dane straddled Jax's lap and grabbed the man's nearly purple cock. He felt Jax's hands on his hips to help steady him and then he was bearing down on the thick flesh that was pressed up against his slick hole.

As Dane's body began pulling Jax in inch by inch, a firm grip closed around his cock and began dragging up and down in rhythm to Dane's motion. Dane closed his eyes as he sank the rest of the way down until he felt Jax's balls pressed against his ass.

"So good," he moaned as the burn intensified and began to change over to pleasure. He managed to force his eyes open and met Jax's intense gaze. Suddenly everything else was gone except for that look in Jax's eyes and the corresponding heat that flooded Dane's system. Dane tried not to believe he was seeing more than desire or need in that haunting gaze because getting his hopes up that Jax was feeling the same things he was feeling was too much to wish for. And he knew what he was feeling was the one thing he'd promised himself he'd never feel again after Isaac's betrayal.

～

Jax could see he was losing Dane to his thoughts so he forced back the overwhelming emotion he'd been struggling with as Dane had welcomed him into his body and yanked Dane's head down for a kiss. The move seemed to do the trick because Dane began moving his body again even as he made love to Jax's mouth. Jax knew he wasn't going to last long thanks to Dane's earlier sensuous torture so he started thrusting up on Dane's downward motion.

Dane's hands clamped down on his shoulders as he began to desperately twist his hips in an effort to take Jax in deeper. But Jax knew there would be no deeper so he increased the leverage by grabbing Dane's ass with both his hands and driving into him over and over. Dane's hand dropped down to stroke his own cock and his head fell back as moans of agony tore from his lips. "Harder," he begged as he viciously pulled and twisted his cock.

Jax held off his orgasm and slammed into Dane several more times until he felt the first spurt of semen hit his chest. It was all he needed to let go of his control and his body snapped back against the couch as his orgasm ripped through him. Dane kept riding him as the waves went on and on and Jax forced his eyes open to watch the last jets of come drip down Dane's cock and over his hand. His own body continued to convulse as Dane's throbbing ass pulsed around him. Dane's hips finally slowed to a gentle rolling motion before stopping all together. Brown eyes clashed with his as a satisfied smile spread over Dane's mouth. Jax knew in that instant that he was in deep shit because there was no longer any doubt that he was completely in love with this man.

CHAPTER 7

"Will you tell me about your brother?"

Dane saw Jax stiffen and he wished the question back. The other man had been sullen and quiet since their interlude on the couch and it was throwing Dane off. He'd asked Jax to join him in the shower but Jax had made an excuse about needing to make a phone call and had disappeared outside. He'd reappeared and helped Dane make dinner but even that had been done mostly in silence. Dane was struggling with his neediness to ask Jax if he'd done something wrong so finding another topic of conversation seemed like the prudent thing to do and he really wanted to know more about Jax's life.

"What do you want to know?"

"Was he older? Younger? Do you have any other brothers or sisters?"

Jax finished the last bit of food on his plate, then took over spoon feeding Emma in her high chair so Dane could work on his dinner. "Ben was younger but only by a minute. We were twins. Fraternal, not identical," he clarified.

"Our sister Jillian is a lot younger – she turned out to be a pleasant surprise for our parents who'd been told they wouldn't be able to have any more kids after Ben and I were born."

"Are your parents still...?"

"Alive? Yeah. They live in Connecticut in the house we grew up in. Jillian's completing her last year of graduate school in Rhode Island."

"Do you get home to see them a lot?"

Jax fell silent for a moment before saying, "Not as much as I probably should. It's been harder since we lost Ben."

Dane wished he could reach out and touch Jax but Jax's earlier withdrawal kept him from doing it.

"Did Ben always know he wanted to go into law enforcement?" Dane asked.

Jax nodded. "We both did. We were the type of twins who did everything together, even after we were old enough to make our own choices. We joined the army together, then the FBI Training Academy. We finally went our separate ways when he decided to move to Chicago and I went to South America."

"You're an FBI agent?" Dane asked in surprise and realized he hadn't taken the time until now to really learn more about this man who'd become so important to him in such a small amount of time. "I thought you worked for a security company?"

"I do. I left the Bureau about a year ago when I realized they weren't going to do anything about Rawlings," Jax responded, his tone going cold.

"You said they were doing surveillance on Rawlings," Dane said.

"Not to get him for his role in what happened to Ben and the others. They wanted the dealer he sold the information to and once they had that guy they were going to offer him immunity so he'd roll on his suppliers. They had no plans to prosecute anyone for the murders and they had no issue with leaving Rhys in prison to rot."

"I'm sorry, Jax."

"My friend got me some contract work for the security company he worked for." Jax refused to meet his gaze when he said, "I used the time between contacts to come up with my own plan for justice for Ben and the others. I spent months traveling back and forth to

Chicago to monitor Rawlings and learn as much about him as I could. His movements, his tastes. After I got what I needed from him, I asked a friend at the FBI to leak the transcripts of the surveillance to the press so the Bureau would be forced to go after the dealer for the murders, but not until I made sure the dealer found out Rawlings had double-crossed him. The dealer took care of Rawlings, the Bureau took care of the dealer." Jax finished feeding Emma and used her bib to wipe her mouth. He leaned down to give her a kiss and smiled when she grabbed his face with her messy hands.

Dane couldn't stop himself from getting up and going around the table. Jax looked up at him curiously but didn't pull away from him when he leaned down to kiss him. "You're an amazing man, Jaxon Reid," Dane said as he pressed another kiss to his lips and then used his thumb to wipe away some of the baby food that was stuck to his cheek. "How about we go for a swim?"

~

*D*ane leaned back against a tree and watched Jax play with Emma in the water. Jax was up to his waist in the cool, clear water in the small pond just a few hundred yards from the house. He'd only agreed to take Emma in the water if Dane stayed on shore and kept Jax's gun handy. The weapon sat next to Dane where he could easily grab it if he needed to, but it was a stark reminder of just how different his and Jax's lives were and the pipe dream he had of being able to have a life with Jax was just that.

At this very moment Jax looked happier and more relaxed than Dane had ever seen him, but Dane still caught him checking their surroundings every couple of minutes. Dane knew Jax did it for his and Emma's sake and he was grateful, but this was also who Jax was and Dane knew the protective man wouldn't be able to give up watching out for others. Dane had nothing that could compete with the adrenaline rush that was the other man's life every day.

Dane knew the prudent thing to do would be to get Jax out of his life sooner rather than later but he also knew in his gut that he wasn't going to let Jax go until he absolutely had to. It would likely end up breaking him but at least he'd have the time they spent together to look back on.

"You going back in?" Jax asked as he came out of the water. Dane admired the way his wet jeans clung to him.

"No, I'm good."

Jax handed him Emma and then pocketed the gun and grabbed his shirt. As they began to walk back to the house, Dane felt the sudden urge to grab Jax's hand but he didn't because that's what couples did and couples were people who had a future together.

"You okay?" Jax asked.

Dane nodded. "Who'd you call earlier today?" he asked.

"My friend at the security firm. I asked him to have our tech people check your phone again for anything unusual."

The reminder that Jax was only here for one reason was brutal but Dane pushed the painful thought away. "Maybe it really was a carjacking and the rest was just some weird coincidence."

"Maybe," Jax agreed.

They both fell silent and Dane felt the tension returning between them. But he couldn't bring himself to ask Jax what was going on so instead he said, "Will you do something for me, Jax?"

"Anything," Jax responded. God, how Dane wished that were true.

"Whenever you're ready to move on, just go. Don't draw it out or make excuses. I'm a big boy and I know this has to end sometime. Just please don't lie to me."

Dane hid his disappointment when all he got in response was a non-committal grunt. He left Jax inside the front door and went to the bathroom to give Emma a quick bath. The little girl's exhaustion was clear because she didn't make the usual fuss about getting out of the tub and her eyes were closed by the time Dane got her into her pajamas and put her in her crib. He left Emma's room and saw that Jax's door was closed. A clear message if he'd ever seen one.

Dane went into his room and closed the door, then came to a stop when he saw Jax leaning against the bedpost. "We need to get a few things straight," he said angrily.

Jax stalked to where Dane stood and grabbed him by the arm and dragged him over to the bed. He pushed Dane onto it and followed him down so that his greater weight held Dane in place for their chat. "That's twice now that you've implied that I'm only here because I have to be. Tell me why."

"Jax, let me up," Dane ordered.

"Not until you talk to me."

"Let me up!" Dane said again, his voice cracking as his anger started to take hold.

Jax pinned Dane's arms when he tried to push him off. "Tell me what happened between this morning and tonight that has you questioning my intentions already."

"No."

"Was it the sex? Was I too rough?" Jax asked as he ran the events of the day through his mind. "Did I hurt you?"

"Let go of me, Jax."

"Please, Dane, talk to me."

Dane closed his eyes and turned his head away. "You wouldn't speak to me," he whispered.

Jax felt like Dane had punched him and he realized how his actions after they'd made love on the couch must have seemed to someone who'd been so coldly betrayed by a man he trusted – a man who'd claimed to love him.

"Dane, I'm sorry," he started to say but Dane began to struggle beneath him.

"Let go!" he shouted and Jax hoped to hell he hadn't woken Emma up because Jax wasn't about to let this go.

"Damn it, just listen!" Jax yelled as he tightened his grip on Dane's arms. "I realized this afternoon that I'm in love with you!" Dane went completely still beneath him. "And I'm scared to death because it's never happened to me before. I needed some time to try and wrap my head around it."

"Jax," Dane began but Jax stopped his words with a kiss.

He pulled back and said, "You don't need to say it back. But I need you to stop punishing me for what Isaac did to you."

"I haven't-"

"You compared me to him last night. Do you remember?"

Dane shook his head.

"After your nightmare you said he was a lot like me." Jax loosened his hold on Dane as the man quieted. "I think you see him whenever you look at me and my guess is that at some point in your relationship he used your insecurities against you and you're waiting for me to do the same thing."

"I loved him," Dane whispered.

"Oh baby, I know that. And he was a lucky man but he should have done better by you." Jax couldn't resist leaning down and kissing Dane again. Some of the tension drained out of him when Dane kissed him back and he released his hold on the other man completely and was rewarded with two strong arms wrapping around his shoulders.

"I can't make you trust me, Dane. But I'm going to trust you not to break my heart the way Isaac broke yours."

Jax sat up, pulling Dane up with him. "I need you, Dane. I need you inside of me," he said softly as he began tugging Dane's shirt off. Dane hesitated for a moment, then reached for Jax and kissed him hard. He let Dane guide him down to the bed and relished the feel of Dane's weight pressing him into the mattress. Firm lips traced his jawline and trailed a path down his neck. Fingers pushed his shirt up to reveal his stomach and a hot tongue began exploring him.

"Take it off," Dane mumbled as he pushed Jax's shirt higher. Jax fumbled with the garment as Dane continued tormenting him with his teeth and tongue and when Dane's hot, wet mouth closed over his nipple, Jax moaned and grabbed Dane's head to keep him there. The same attention was given to the other side and then Dane was closing his mouth over Jax's again. Dane reared back and worked the rest of Jax's clothes off. As he crawled back up the length of Jax's body, Jax spread his legs to make room for him and sighed when the fabric of Dane's jeans brushed over his sensitive cock.

Jax closed his eyes and just enjoyed the sensation of being loved.

Dane left no place on him untouched and when he finally reached Jax's cock he worshipped every inch of it before drawing the entire length deep into his mouth. Jax managed to open his eyes long enough to watch Dane bobbing up and down on him as his cheeks hollowed over and over again and he couldn't help but reach his hand down and close it over the hand Dane had splayed across his abdomen. Dane instantly intertwined their fingers.

"Dane, I'm close," Jax managed to get out as Dane increased his suction. His words had no impact and before he could say anything else, Dane was swallowing around his length as a finger brushed over his hole. Jax cried out as his orgasm caught him off guard and he watched Dane swallow his release. His body melted from the pleasure and he felt drained as Dane released him and climbed up his body. When Dane kissed him, Jax eagerly licked the remaining proof of his orgasm from Dane's lips.

Dane leaned back and traced his fingers around Jax's mouth and then dragged his thumb over his lips. "It's too much," he whispered as he met Jax's gaze. Jax had no idea what he meant and didn't get to ask because Dane began kissing him again, then sat up and worked the remainder of his clothes off. Jax pulled the lube and a condom out of the nightstand.

"Jax," Dane said, a fine tremor shaking through his voice.

"Yeah?"

"I've only done this a couple times," he said. "I haven't been with many men and most of them didn't want me to…"

"I want this, Dane. I've been dreaming about it since the first time you kissed me."

Dane looked taken aback and it was yet another reminder that between his father and the men in his life, Dane's self-confidence had taken a brutal hit. Dane leaned over him and brushed a soft kiss over his lips.

"Don't let me hurt you, Jax," he whispered and Jax couldn't help but wonder if Dane was referring to the present moment or what would come tomorrow. Jax didn't have much time to consider it as Dane rolled him to his stomach and a big hand held him open as slick fingers began probing his hole. He bit into his lip to stifle his moan as a finger pressed inside of him. Bottoming hadn't been something he'd done often but he hadn't lied when he'd said he dreamed of Dane doing this to him. More lube was worked into his body and the sting intensified as little starbursts of pleasure began to dance behind his eyes. A second finger joined the first and Dane flicked his wrist, twisting the probing digits.

"Please, Dane," Jax said as he dropped his forehead against the mattress. Relief went through him as he heard the condom wrapper being torn open but Dane's fingers continued to probe him. Dane slowly pulled them out and settled his palm on Jax's lower back and he tensed when he felt the broad head of Dane's dick begin stretching him. Jax bore down on Dane and moaned when his hole collapsed and Dane easily slid the rest of the way in.

"Oh God," Jax hissed against his arm as the burning pressure expanded out to the rest of his body.

"Are you okay?" Dane asked as both hands stroked up Jax's back.

Jax was too overcome to speak so he nodded and reached back with his arm to touch Dane's thigh. He was glad when Dane got the silent message and began to slowly rock in and out of him.

～

Sweat dripped down Dane's forehead as he carefully pushed back into Jax and felt his inner walls ripple around him. Jax's ass was an amazing sight on its own but to see his cock sliding in and out of the powerful man beneath him and hearing Jax's little grunts every time he did it had Dane trying to stave off his orgasm. The last thing he'd expected tonight was Jax's admission of love and truth be told, he was doing everything he could to keep it out of his immediate thoughts because he wanted this moment to be exactly what it was – him and Jax the way they were meant to be. There wasn't any of the bullshit that acted as a filter in his head whenever the words he wanted to hear were spoken to him. No, it was two men sharing in the pleasure their bodies could bring. If he let it be anything more than that, he'd just fuck it up like he did everything else.

Dane ran his hands over the tattoo on Jax's shoulder and followed it down to his spine. He kept up his slow, deep rhythm as he traced his fingers down Jax's back and over his ass. He spread Jax's cheeks so he could watch himself disappear in and out of the other man. When he felt that familiar prickle along the back of his neck, he knew instantly what it meant and glanced up to confirm that Jax was indeed watching him. He'd thought taking Jax from behind would make it easier to control his fierce desire but now he wanted nothing more than to watch Jax come apart beneath him.

Dane lowered his body along Jax's back and humped into him as he leaned down and kissed Jax, then traced the shell of his ear with his tongue. "I need to see you," he said softly before he forced himself to pull out of Jax and turn him over. He missed the man's heat for even the few seconds it took to get him in position and he fumbled to get back inside of Jax before the cold that he knew would eventually come would overtake this moment. Jax sighed when Dane resumed his pace and his legs came up to wrap around Dane.

"Touch yourself," Dane heard himself order and wondered where the huskiness in his voice had come from.

Jax did as he was told and began stroking his cock to match Dane's thrusting. "Harder," Dane said as he pulled Jax's ass up higher so he could get deeper. He slammed into Jax hard once and then did a few shallow thrusts. He repeated the move again and again, reveling in Jax's grunts as he began to anticipate the powerful plunges. Jax's jerking of his cock became more frantic as Dane increased the pace and began hammering in and out of him.

Dane suddenly pulled all the way out and tapped the head of his cock over Jax's sensitive hole several times before shoving himself back inside.

"Fuck, yes!" Jax shouted when Dane did it again and pre-come began leaking from the head of Jax's dick. Dane slammed into him again and ran his fingers over the head of Jax's cock and collected some of the fluid. He shoved his fingers into Jax's mouth and watched as he eagerly sucked on them.

Dane kept up his pounding as he leaned down to kiss Jax and the tangy flavor set off shockwaves of delight inside him. He shoved Jax's hand away from his cock and took over the merciless jerking as he pummeled Jax over and over. Skin slapped against skin and their moans and cries of pleasure mingled together as they reached the edge.

"Harder, Dane. Fuck me harder!" Jax shouted as he grabbed the rails of the wooden headboard above his head.

Dane was ruthless after that, all fear of hurting the man beneath him gone as he pushed them higher and higher. As the bed shook, Dane forced his eyes open and saw Jax watching him, eyes bright with emotion, mouth open but no sound coming out. Suddenly it wasn't enough anymore and Dane dropped down onto Jax and wrapped his free hand around the back of Jax's neck and lifted his head until their foreheads met.

"Tell me again, Jax, please," he begged.

Jax's arms went around him and drew him down. "I love you, Dane," he whispered against Dane's ear and Dane screamed in pleasure as he came. Jax's body clamped down on his dick as Jax shouted his name and then the words came again. Jax kept repeating them and Dane's body jerked every time the beautiful words washed over him. Jax's release was hot between them and Dane closed his eyes as his own cock twitched one more time inside of Jax before everything went dark.

CHAPTER 8

*J*ax felt his gut clench as he watched Dane moving around the kitchen. He'd hoped his admission of love would bring him some measure of peace, but the exact opposite had occurred and Dane couldn't sit still to save his life. Nor would he connect with Jax for more than a moment at a time and that was usually a random question about their plans for the day or what he wanted of dinner. There'd been a small part of him that had hoped Dane would say the words back to him, especially after Dane had begged Jax to tell him he loved him again last night but Dane hadn't even acknowledged anything about what had happened between them. The sex with Dane got better and better every time but it seemed the more in sync their bodies became, the wider their emotional connection grew.

Dane's phone rang and Jax couldn't help but glance down on the table where it sat near Dane's nearly full cup of coffee. He physically flinched when Gray Hawthorne's name appeared on the screen.

"Who is it?" Dane asked as he began filling the dishwasher.

Jax shifted Emma in his arms, picked up the phone and took it over to Dane who frowned when he saw who was calling. His eyes shot up to Jax's.

"It's fine, take it," Jax said. "I'm going to go change her," he said as he left the kitchen. Pain lanced through him when he heard Dane answer.

Jax got Emma cleaned up and put a new diaper on her. Never in a million years had he thought he'd be changing a baby's diaper. Of course, there'd been a lot of firsts for him in the last couple of weeks since meeting Dane.

"I'm getting better, huh?" he asked Emma as he picked her up and reached into her crib for one of her toys. It was some kind of strange animal that rattled but also made a weird crunching sound whenever Emma squeezed its limbs. He'd come to learn it was her favorite.

"He invited us to dinner," Jax heard Dane say behind him. "I told him maybe some other time."

For some reason Dane's words didn't make Jax feel any better, probably because it sounded like Dane had declined more to please him than anything else.

"I was wondering if we could go into town for a bit. I was hoping to talk to Wendy and see if she was interested in becoming my tech when I open my practice."

"Sure," Jax said, forcing his voice to be more casual than he was feeling.

"Damn it, Jax, what do you want from me?" he heard Dane ask in frustration.

Jax sighed. "I want you to not have to ask me that, Dane. It's not about what I want." He turned around and handed Emma over to Dane. "I'll meet you by the car."

~

*D*ane put Emma down in her crib as that familiar wave of agitation overcame him and his father's voice pierced his brain, the cruel words taunting him. He closed Emma's door and then went into his own room and locked the door. The pain in his head increased until it felt like someone was stabbing needles through his skull. Why wouldn't Jax just tell him what he wanted?

What were the right words to say? Why couldn't he make this fucking work?

Weak.

Dane shoved his fists into his eyes.

Pathetic.

"Stop!" he shouted as he leaned back against the wall.

Fucking pussy.

Something shattered and then a blaring noise surged through his head.

Love you, Doc.

Dane heard his name being called but he was too tired to care and he dropped to the floor as the needles began to pierce his flesh.

❧

"*D*ane"! Jax screamed as he flew up the stairs, ignoring the blaring alarm. He could hear Emma screaming and he threw open her door. Relief went through him at the sight of her unharmed in her crib. Tears were flowing down her red cheeks as her shrill cries pierced the air.

"Dane!" he shouted again and pure terror went through him at the sight of Dane's closed door. He tried the knob but the door didn't budge. He threw all his weight against it and it easily broke free of the frame. Horror slammed into him at the sight of Dane on his knees on a bed of glass at the base of his dresser. The mirror frame attached to the dresser stood empty except for a few pieces of glass hanging along the edges. Dane was clutching the remains of a small metal lamp in his hand and Jax recognized it as the lamp that used to sit on top of the dresser.

"Jax!" someone called from downstairs as the front door crashed open. He recognized the voice and pushed back his shock at seeing his friend appearing in Dane's doorway.

"Cade, get the baby out of the house. Across the hall! And turn off the alarm-307175!"

His friend didn't hesitate and disappeared into Emma's room.

"Dane?" Jax called as he reached Dane's side and plucked him from the shards of glass. He was grateful to see that Dane at least had shoes on but blood was forming in small pools beneath his jeans from where Dane had been kneeling in the glass. He got them both clear of the debris and settled Dane against his body.

The blaring of the alarm went silent and seconds later Dane's phone rang. Knowing it was the security service, Jax fished the phone out of Dane's pocket and answered it. He rattled off the password and told the operator that a broken glass had triggered the alarm before throwing the phone aside.

"Dane, baby, talk to me," he said as he rocked Dane back and forth.

"Make it stop, Jax," he whispered against Jax's chest. "Please make it stop."

"I will, baby. I promise," he said as he wrapped his arms around Dane.

~

*D*ane crawled out of his bed and made it to the bathroom just in time to empty the contents of his stomach into the toilet. A cool washcloth was pressed against his forehead as a warm hand settled on his back but he pushed them both away and climbed to his feet. He rinsed out his mouth, ignoring Jax's worried look. He was careful to avoid the mirror above the sink and quickly dried off his face and left the bathroom.

"Where is she?" he asked.

"Callan, Finn and Rhys agreed to watch her tonight."

"Good," he said quietly as he came to a stop in Emma's doorway. At least he hadn't done anything in front of his daughter.

Dane went down the stairs and into the kitchen, his eyes searching every countertop. He came to a stop when he saw a dark haired man sitting at the kitchen table, a cup of coffee in front of him. A second cup sat in front of the chair opposite him. Jax's cup, likely. Sure, because every discussion about one's crazy lover went better if you had a good cup of coffee in your hand.

"Dane, this is Cade. He's the friend I was telling you about from Seattle."

Perfect. Fucking perfect.

"How you feeling?" Cade asked, his sharp eyes quickly sizing him up. Dane knew exactly what the stunning man saw and he ignored the outstretched hand as he went to search the desk against the wall.

"What are you looking for?" Jax asked

"My phone."

"It's here," Jax said as he held up Dane's cell phone.

"Give it to me," he snapped.

"Cade, give us a minute?" Jax said, his eyes never leaving Dane's.

Cade shuffled past them and disappeared outside and Dane finally realized it was nearly dark. He'd been out all day.

"Give me the phone," he said again and held out his hand.

"Who are you calling?" Jax asked.

"None of your business."

He wasn't surprised when Jax grabbed his arm so hard it nearly hurt. "None of my business? You dare say that to me after what happened today?" Jax hurled his phone across the room and it hit the wall with a resounding thud. "What the fuck is so important that you can't take five minutes to explain to me what the hell happened to you this morning?"

Dane felt nothing as he raised his eyes and simply said, "I need to call Emma's grandmother to come get her."

❧

"I thought you weren't in touch with your parents," Jax said, his fingers biting mercilessly into Dane's arm. Of all the ways he'd thought his conversation with Dane would go, this hadn't even been on his radar.

"Isaac's mother."

"Emma's fine spending the night at the ranch."

"I'm not talking about tonight."

Dane pulled free of him and went to get the phone. From his

97

annoyed curse Jax knew he'd broken it. His affect was starting to worry Jax more than his breakdown had.

"What are you saying?"

Dane began rifling through an address book he pulled out of the desk drawer. "Belinda has wanted Emma since the day Isaac died. She'll take good care of her."

Jax reached Dane in three sides and slammed him back against the wall. "What the fuck is wrong with you?"

Dane was eerily calm as he remained still in Jax's grip. "It's for the best."

The man sounded like a fucking robot. Jax began to tremble as he realized his Dane was gone. He didn't know this man.

"Dane," he whispered as he gentled his hold on Dane and pressed their foreheads together. "Please don't do this to me. Not when I just found you."

He covered Dane's mouth with his but the man didn't move, didn't even flinch. He forced Dane's head up so that their eyes met and he said, "Nothing's changed for me. I'm still here. I still love you. You could burn this place to the fucking ground and I will still love you. You can curse me to hell and back a thousand times over and I will still love you. Do you hear me?" he said harshly as he kissed Dane again.

Jax felt a tremor go through Dane. "Come back to me," he urged as he kissed him again and tears pricked the backs of his eyes when he felt Dane soften beneath him and open his mouth. He pressed his advantage and kissed Dane thoroughly.

"I've never done anything like that before," Dane said against his lips. "I kept hearing their voices and I just wanted to make it stop."

"I know. We'll figure it out."

"It's too hard, Jax. I don't know how to make this work. I don't know the right things to say." Dane's fingers bit into his skin as he whispered, "I could have hurt Emma."

"No. You know that's not true."

"But I don't. I don't know anything anymore."

Jax pulled Dane against him. "We'll figure it out," he repeated, hoping to hell Dane couldn't hear the uncertainty in his voice.

~

"*D*o you think I'm crazy?"

Jax tightened his arm around Dane's waist and drew him closer. He was glad when Dane's hand closed over his. They'd been laying on Dane's bed for the better part of an hour and Dane's silence had Jax worrying that he was slipping away again. "No. I think you've had a lot to deal with lately."

"Why do you want to be with me?"

"Because I think you're one of the strongest, kindest men I've ever met. You're an amazing friend and no child could ask for a better father."

Dane was silent for a long time again before he said, "She's not mine."

"Yes she is."

"Isaac was her biological father."

"She's yours, Dane." Jax leaned down to press a kiss against the back of Dane's neck. "I thought you and Isaac didn't want to know."

"We didn't. Isaac's mother sued me for custody after Isaac died and the court ordered a paternity test." Jax was surprised at the revelation.

"Why did she want custody?"

"It was just her and Isaac after his father died when he was little. They were really close and it was hard for her to let him go. She never really liked me much – she told me once that Isaac could do better."

Jax forced himself not to let Dane feel the anger simmering through him. He wondered if there had been any people in Dane's life who had accepted him for who he was.

"I was the one who had to tell her he was gone. She said it was my fault. She said he wouldn't have even been there if I hadn't thrown our marriage away. I guess he didn't tell her the reason it was over. She said I didn't deserve Emma and that she'd be better off with her."

"So she took you to court?"

Dane nodded. "She said since I was planning on filing for divorce that I had no legal standing to keep Emma."

"She had to have known the courts wouldn't buy that argument," Jax said.

"I think she was just trying to wear me down. The legal battle drained most of my savings and I ended up having to sell the house Isaac and I bought to make ends meet. By the time it was over I just needed to start over."

"What made you pick Dare?"

Dane snuggled back against him even further. "Isaac's aunt and uncle on his father's side owned this place. They died about a year ago and left it to him. I liked the idea of bringing Emma up in a small town and I knew I wouldn't have to spend too much to get my practice up and running because his aunt and uncle had built a small boarding facility which I could easily convert."

"Smart," Jax said.

"What if I can't figure out what's happening to me, Jax? If you hadn't been here today…"

"But I was. The what-ifs don't matter."

Dane turned in his arms. "You have a whole other life that I can't compete with."

Jax shook his head slowly as he reached out to run his fingers through Dane's hair. "Don't you get it yet, Dane?" Jax leaned down and kissed him. "The life I had before you and Emma is what can't compete."

~

"*M*orning."

Dane jumped at the strange voice and then remembered Jax's friend. The man was sitting in the same exact spot at the kitchen table as the night before with yet another cup of coffee in front of him.

"Morning," Dane returned. "It's Cade, right?" The man nodded and his penetrating gaze had Dane shifting uncomfortably. "Jax is still asleep."

"There's coffee," he said as he motioned to the pot. The last thing Dane wanted to do was try to have a friendly chat with the gorgeous stranger who'd witnessed his complete humiliation yesterday. The one who was even now judging him and likely finding him lacking.

"Thanks." He had no idea why he was thanking the guy for the coffee from his own damn coffee maker but what else was he supposed to say? What he really wanted to know was what the man was doing here. And to his shame, he really wanted to know what the man was to Jax. Friends meant different things to different people. "Did Jax ask you to come?"

"Not in so many words," Cade answered non-committedly.

What the hell did that mean? Dane forced a sip of coffee down and studied the other man. The guy was fucking huge, taller than Jax even and oozed confidence and power. A navy blue T-shirt hugged his ripped torso and his thick thighs bulged against his tight jeans. He saw a tattoo peeking out underneath one sleeve and another at the base of his neck.

"Jax said you work for the same security company in Seattle?" Dane said, hoping to get the conversation onto an easy topic – one that wouldn't have Cade looking at him like he was a bug he wanted to stomp with his huge combat boot.

Cade nodded. "Barretti Security Group."

"What kind of work do you do?"

"Personal protection mostly. Some PI stuff. The firm specializes in information security too but Jax and I focus on the protection side of things." Cade took a long, slow sip of his coffee before saying, "It's a good fit for Jax because he's always had a thing for protecting those that were weaker than him."

Dane didn't miss the dig but he wasn't about to take the bait. "How long have you known him?"

"A while. He and Ben and I served together in Iraq. It was their first deployment, my second. We connected again after I finished my third tour. Jax was doing some undercover work for the Bureau in South America."

"What kind of work?"

"His unit focused mostly on human trafficking."

Dane shuddered at the horrible things Jax must have witnessed. "Jesus," he whispered.

"He was undercover for two years. Helped break up an entire syndicate that was worth hundreds of millions of dollars. Saved countless lives."

Dane leaned back against the counter and felt his insides go numb because he realized the direction Cade was heading.

"You know the kind of fortitude it takes to live a lie for two years? To pretend to be something you're not and have your life depend on being able to maintain that lie?"

Dane nearly laughed because he did know. He'd been pretending since the day he walked out of his parents' house that he was everything they said he wasn't. But the few men he'd been with had seen through him and wielded his self-doubt like a weapon against him. And near the end with Isaac he'd been willing to twist himself into anything Isaac wanted to keep his love, but even that hadn't been enough. And now his desire to be enough for Jax was causing him to implode.

"Two years and he didn't break. Not once. But you. You managed to break him in less than a week," Cade said coldly. Dane flinched at the anger he heard in the other man's voice. "He told me you thought he was shit."

Dane felt tears sting his eyes. He knew Jax had felt that way because Jax had admitted it. It had been foolish to think that Dane could be forgiven for inflicting such cruelty on the man. It had been foolish to think a lot of things.

"He deserves better than you," Cade muttered in disgust.

"Cade!"

Dane didn't bother to lift his head at the sound of Jax's voice. But he did step in front of Jax when he started to go after his friend.

"Don't." He let his hand rest on Jax's chest. "Just don't." He glanced over his shoulder at Cade who'd stood at Jax's advance. "Would you give us a minute, please?"

Cade kicked the chair aside and stormed out the back door.

"Dane," Jax started to say but Dane put his thumb on Jax's lips to silence him. He trailed his finger over Jax's mouth.

"Do you remember when you said you were trusting me not to break your heart?"

Jax nodded.

"I wanted so badly to tell you that I wouldn't, but I knew it was something I couldn't promise. Give your trust to someone who's earned it, Jax. Love someone who's worthy of you. We both know I'm not that man."

Dane tried to step past Jax but wasn't surprised when Jax grabbed him. He expected the man to yell at him or curse him or flat out refuse to let him go but instead he heard, "Do you love me, Dane?" The fingers biting into his arms loosened and moved up to hold his face. "Tell me the truth."

Jax held his head so he couldn't look away. He wasn't even sure he managed to get the word out until he saw Jax's eyes widen with pain and then those big hands were releasing him. Jax stepped out of his way and Dane allowed himself one final look at the beautiful man as he left the kitchen, grabbing his car keys as he went. He could now add liar to his long list of deficiencies.

CHAPTER 9

*N*o.

Agony pierced Jax's chest as he crumpled into the nearest chair. He would have bet his life that Dane would have answered his question with a yes and that's all he would have needed. The rest was just noise that he would have found a way to work through with Dane. He'd been willing to fight for as long as it took to show Dane that he was here to stay, but if Dane didn't share his feelings than what difference would it make?

"I heard his car leave."

All the rage he'd felt towards Cade when he heard his friend disparaging his lover had faded and he was left with a sense of betrayal unlike any he'd ever known.

"Why?" he managed to choke out as Cade leaned back against the refrigerator.

"The guy's fucked up, Jax!"

Jax reared out of the chair and slammed his fist into Cade's jaw. Cade managed to catch himself before he fell.

"I'm in love with him you fucking asshole!"

Cade stroked a hand over his jaw. "He thinks he's better than you. You said so yourself!"

"Jesus, fucking Christ!" Jax shouted as he turned away from Cade before he did something to his friend that he'd truly regret. "I told you that two weeks ago. Did it ever occur to you that things might have changed since then?"

Cade pushed off the refrigerator, his eyes flashing. "You called me two days ago and I heard it in your fucking voice even then, Jax! And it's not like he was standing here defending how he felt about you!"

"That's because you did what every other man in his life has done to him. You sought out his insecurities and you exploited them! His father, his lovers, even his fucking husband messed with his head for years by telling him he wasn't good enough and you just did the same goddamn thing! And what you heard in my voice was me trying to deal with the fact that I was in love with someone for the first time in my life and scared shitless that he might not love me back."

"But yesterday..."

"Yesterday happened because I pushed him too hard! He was trying to please me and I got upset because I didn't want him making decisions based on what he thought I wanted. And instead of talking to him about it I walked away!"

Cade opened his mouth to say something then promptly snapped it shut again. He went pale and began searching his pockets for his beloved cigarettes – the ones he'd given up months ago. It had always been Cade's tell and Jax realized his friend was finally registering what he'd done.

"Where would he go?" Cade asked. "Maybe I can talk to him..."

Jax sighed and sank down into one of the chairs. "Just go home, Cade."

"No, I can fix this..."

"He doesn't want me. If he did he would have fought for me...for us."

Cade sank down in the chair across from him. Cade had always been an indomitable force of nature who bulldozed his way through life and took what he wanted so it was strange to see him so dazed.

"What are you going to do?" Cade asked quietly.

"What I should have done from the beginning. My job."

~

"*H*ey, how's it going?" Callan asked as Dane got out of his SUV. "Rhys and Finn are still up at the house with Emma."

Callan must have sensed Dane's agitation because he put down the saddle he'd been about to place on his horse. "What's going on?"

Dane paced the small barn aisle until he felt Callan's strong hand closing over his shoulder and pressing him back against one of the stall doors. "Talk to me, Dane."

"Did Jax tell you what happened yesterday? What I did?"

"He just said something came up and asked us to keep an eye on Emma for you for the night." Callan's calm voice was soothing and Dane felt himself marginally relax.

"I have a favor to ask."

"Okay."

"Can Emma and I stay here for a little while? In the house next to yours?"

"Of course."

Dane waited for the inevitable questions but they didn't come and he knew by looking at Callan that it wasn't because he didn't care. It was in the quiet man's nature not to push – it was what made him so good with the abused and neglected horses he often worked with.

"How about we go for a ride?" Callan said.

Dane really wanted to see Emma but Callan had picked up on his need to get himself under control. He managed a nod and within ten minutes he was sitting on Kirby's back, the old Pinto moving at a snail's pace next to Callan's mount who fidgeted nervously.

"Why did you wait so long to tell Finn you loved him?" Dane heard himself asking before he realized how inappropriate the question was. He started to apologize for even asking it but Callan cut him off.

"Because I was afraid of what I'd lose."

"Your family?"

Callan nodded. "But it was more than that. I didn't think Finn would love me if I abandoned my family for a life with him. And I knew I couldn't ask him to give up his future for a half-life with me."

"Stuck between a rock and a hard place," Dane observed dryly.

"That's what I thought at the time. But I realize now it was Finn's choice to make, not mine. He loved me despite my flaws - real or imagined - and it should have been his choice whether or not he wanted to make a life with me."

Dane fell silent as he remembered how Jax had said he'd love him no matter what he did. He tried to think back to his early years with Isaac and couldn't remember a time where the man who would be his husband had said anything beyond 'I love you.' Whenever Dane had started to feel needy and insecure, Isaac had been dismissive at best – had told Dane he was being ridiculous. But Jax had called him on it and talked it out instead of brushing him off.

"Callan, I need you to do something else for me," Dane said.

Callan must have heard the seriousness in his tone because he pulled his horse to a halt and Kirby automatically stopped too.

"I need to know that you guys will look out for Emma if something happens to me."

Callan tensed and his horse shifted. He automatically put a hand on the animal's neck to soothe it. "Tell me what's going on, Dane."

Dane dragged in a breath and then told Callan about the incident the day before with the mirror.

"That's why I need to stay here. I can't risk Emma being alone with me if something like that happens again."

Callan looked at him long and hard and then he shook his head. But instead of answering Dane, he asked, "What happened between you and Jax?"

Dane pulled his eyes away from Callan's and scanned the valley ahead of them. "It's not going to work out."

"I saw the way he looked at you. He's in love with you."

Dane closed his eyes as a wave of pain went through him. "Will you be there for Emma or not?" When Callan didn't answer, Dane felt the last of his energy drain out of him and he picked up Kirby's reins with the intent to steer the horse back to the barn. Callan leaned down and grabbed the horse's bridle.

"We will always be there for Emma. And you. But don't for one second ask me to believe you would ever hurt that kid," Callan said harshly.

Completely done, Dane climbed off the horse. He had no idea how long of a walk it was back to the barn but he really didn't give a shit.

"You're one of the bravest men I know, Dane. So why are you running away?"

A harsh laugh escaped Dane and he spun around on his heel. Callan had dismounted as well and was just a few steps behind him, leading the two horses. "Brave? Are you fucking kidding me?"

"Strong too."

Dane's gut clenched at the words and he felt tears sting his eyes. "Not you too, Callan."

"Not me what?"

Dane shook his head. "Don't you lie to me too."

"Is that what you think Jax is doing? Lying to you?"

Dane turned and began walking again.

"Do you?" Callan nearly shouted.

"I don't know, okay? I don't fucking know."

"You want to know why I think you're brave?" Callan called.

Dane stopped but didn't turn.

"The day of the shooting."

"I froze," Dane automatically said. "I couldn't do anything."

He felt Callan come to a stop behind him. "That's not true. There was a point where I was calling for you because Finn was down and I saw you look at your daughter and then Finn and I knew. I knew how badly you wanted to go to her. But you chose Finn."

"He needed me."

"But you needed Emma."

It was true. He'd never needed anything more in that moment then to hold his child.

"And you had to have been scared shitless trying to help Finn but you took charge and you did it. The doctors said the bullet nicked an artery and if you hadn't clamped it..." Callan's voice grew thick with emotion. "You saved his life, Dane."

"I did what anyone with the right training would have done," he said quietly.

"You saved his life," Callan repeated firmly. "Rhys told me what you did in the hardware store for him and Finn. How many people stood around and watched that clerk treat Finn and Rhys like dirt? You stepped up when you didn't have to."

Dane fell silent as his insides churned.

"And my God, Dane, you're raising a baby by yourself. And she's happy, Dane – she's happy because you've loved her so well."

He felt Callan take his hand and put Kirby's reins in it. "Don't make the same mistake I did. If you love him, trust him to choose the life he wants. Maybe he'll choose you, maybe he won't. But know that you're strong enough to deal with whatever he decides."

~

"*R*hys, we're fine. Go get what you need," Dane said as he got Emma out of the car seat.

"You'll stay in the bookstore?"

"Yes," Dane said with an exasperated sigh. As much as he appreciated Rhys taking the time to play bodyguard for the last two weeks, he was growing tired of the hovering.

"I'll be five minutes," Rhys promised.

"We'll be here."

Rhys gave him another hard look before turning and heading down the sidewalk towards the sheriff's station.

"Dr. Winters, how are you this fine morning?" he heard Harriet Greene say from behind him.

"Good, Mrs. Greene. How are you?"

"I'm off to feed my babies," she responded as she held up a bag of bread. He must have looked confused because she said, "Don't look at me like I should be taking tours of the nearest funny farm. Ducks, Dr. Winters. I'm off to feed the ducks."

"Right," he said with a smile.

"Emma, would you like to come see the ducks?" Mrs. Greene cooed as she held out her arms.

Dane hesitated even as Emma reached for the woman.

"No worries, Doctor. You'll be able to see us the whole time from the window," she said as she motioned to the small park in the town square across from the bookstore. He could see a few people milling about and sitting on benches and there was a small flock of ducks along with their babies near the edge of the water.

"I'll just be a few minutes," he said as he handed Emma over.

"No rush," Mrs. Greene said dismissively as she walked across the street. Dane waited until she was sitting comfortably on a park bench surrounded by birds before he went into the bookstore. He went to the children's section and started picking out a few more books, willing his brain not to drift to thoughts of Jax. He hadn't seen the other man since the morning he'd told him he didn't love him and left the house. By the time he had returned the next day to get some fresh clothes and some of Emma's things, the house was eerily silent and the only proof that Jax had ever been there was the alarm that had been engaged when he walked in the door.

As each day passed, he kept hoping the painful need for Jax would ease and he could get on with his life but he was beginning to suspect the dull ache in his heart would be there until the day he died. And while he hadn't heard his father's cruel taunts or dreamed of Isaac's lifeless eyes since he'd walked away from Jax, his torment hadn't ended because now all he saw was Jax's wide smile as he played with Emma. All he felt was the whisper of Jax's gentle touch and all he heard were Jax's declarations of love.

"Hey, Dane."

Dane looked up at the sound of the familiar voice and nodded at Gray. "Hi."

"No ladybugs today?" Gray asked as he glanced at the book Dane had been flipping through.

Dane laughed but it sounded hollow even to his own ears. "Not today."

"Where's Jax?"

A sharp pain went through him at the question and he knew he wouldn't be able to answer so he just shook his head.

"Sorry," Gray said gently. "Seemed like a smart guy."

The jab actually irritated Dane and he said, "He is."

"Not if he walked away from you, he isn't," Gray responded. "Let me know if you ever want to take me up on my dinner invite," the man said as he began to walk away.

"Gray, I'm not looking to start anything up," he said awkwardly.

Gray studied him for a moment before saying, "I knew that the second I saw the way you looked at him." Gray smiled sadly and said, "Life's too fucking short, Dane. Grab onto the things that mean the most to you and don't let go."

With that, Gray left and Dane tried to focus on the book in his hand but gave up and put it back on the shelf. He'd been kidding himself to think he could get his life back to normal because the life he'd had before Jax hadn't even been that. He'd been surviving and that was it. And it just wasn't enough anymore.

Dane put the rest of the books he had tucked under his arm down and left the bookstore. He pulled out his phone and sent a quick text letting Rhys know he was in the park and then tucked the phone back in his jacket. His eyes scanned the area around the small pond and a niggle of fear went through him when he saw that the bench Mrs. Greene had been sitting on was empty.

A loud scream pierced the air and he tracked the sound to the far edge of the park. He began running as his brain tried to process what he was seeing. Mrs. Greene lay on the ground at the bottom of a small hill that led up to the street. Had she fallen? He scanned the surrounding ground around her for Emma.

"Stop her!" Mrs. Greene screamed. When she saw him running towards her she pointed up towards the top of the hill and said, "She took her! She took Emma!"

Dane's lungs burned as he flew past Mrs. Greene and dashed up the hill. He heard Emma crying before he saw her and finally located his daughter in the arms of a woman who was running down the sidewalk.

"Stop!" he screamed. He was within feet of the woman when she suddenly turned and pointed a gun at him.

"Belinda?" he said in shock as he recognized Isaac's mother.

"Stay back!" she shouted as she waved the gun at him. She looked nothing like the regal, put-together socialite he remembered. Her usually coiffed hair lay limply around her gaunt face and her frantic eyes darted all around her as she clutched Emma to her. She began backing away from him and towards a car parked at the curb. He slowly moved forward every time she took her eyes off him long enough to search out the car.

"I told you to stay back!" she screamed when she realized he was closer to her now than he had been a few moments earlier.

"Belinda, what are you doing?" he asked as panic welled inside of him. She was waving the gun so much that he feared it would discharge and hit his daughter.

Suddenly Belinda's eyes tracked over his shoulder and the gun was directed at something behind him.

"Put it down," he heard that strong, familiar voice say and a combination of fear and relief went through him.

He watched as Belinda's gun slowly moved off him and he realized Jax was drawing her fire away by moving off to the side. "Belinda, please, you're scaring Emma," he said softly.

A horrified expression crossed Belinda's features and she glanced down at Emma and began trying to soothe her. He used the temporary distraction to glance at Jax who had his gun pointed right at Belinda's head. Dane knew Jax had the shot he needed to end this but instead of pulling the trigger, he gave Dane a subtle nod.

"She likes that song you used to sing Isaac when he was little," Dane said quietly and Belinda snapped her eyes up, her gaze darting between him and Jax. Thankfully, her gun remained pointed at the ground.

"Isaac tried to teach it to me but I could never remember the words."

Dane saw a flash of pain go through Belinda at the mention of her son but then her eyes dropped back to Emma and she began to softly sing. He was glad when Emma quieted and he saw Belinda smile as she sang the final words. A glance over his shoulder showed that several people had collected on the other side of the park and were watching the scene unfold. Gray was at the base of the hill comforting Mrs. Greene and Rhys and Sheriff Granger, both armed, were at the far corner of the street.

"Isaac was afraid of the dark so I'd sing to him until he fell asleep every night," Belinda whispered.

"He was lucky to have you."

Belinda glanced up at him with watery eyes. "I miss him."

"Me too," Dane admitted. "But he wouldn't want this, Belinda. You know that."

She nodded and then reached down to kiss Emma on the forehead. "I didn't mean for it to go this far," she said.

"You hired those men to go after Dane, didn't you?" he heard Jax ask.

"They weren't supposed to hurt him," she said desperately. "They were just supposed to find him and take Emma when he was distracted."

"Lady, you can't be that naïve," Jax snapped.

"Belinda," Dane said gently, needing to get the focus back on Emma. "None of that matters. What matters is that Emma needs you in her life."

Tears began to fall down Belinda's face. "I'm sorry, Dane. I'm sorry I blamed you for what happened. I spoiled Isaac terribly after his father died and sometimes he made bad choices."

"He was a good man, Belinda," Dane said simply.

Belinda nodded and finally lowered the gun. She carefully placed it on the sidewalk and then walked up to him. She gave Emma one more kiss before handing his daughter to him and then she stepped back as Sherriff Granger moved in.

Dane stifled a cry of relief at the feel of Emma in his arms and he held her close as he watched Belinda being escorted to the police station. As the adrenaline began to wear off, his entire body started to shake and he wished in that moment that a pair of strong arms would wrap around him and tell him everything was okay. But he knew before he even turned to look that Jax was already gone.

CHAPTER 10

"I'm sorry, Sir. I'm afraid I can't give you that information," the receptionist said politely. "But if you'd like, I can call Mr. Reid and let him know you're trying to reach him," she offered.

Dane glanced around the immaculate lobby and bit back his disappointment. He knew that getting Jax's address from the company he worked for would be a long shot but he also knew that showing up unannounced was likely his only hope of getting Jax to listen to him.

"Hey Bridget," a young man said as he entered the lobby and began walking towards the side door.

"Good afternoon, Mr. Bradshaw," the receptionist said.

"Are you ever going to call me Logan, Bridget?"

"Of course, Mr. Bradshaw," the woman said with a smile.

The man chuckled and began to open the door that Dane assumed led to the offices, but he stopped when his eyes spotted him and Emma.

"Everything okay here?" he asked.

"This is Dr. Winters. He was looking for Mr. Reid," the receptionist said.

Dane picked up Emma's car seat off the floor and said, "Thanks for your time," to the receptionist.

"Are you Dane?"

Dane stopped with his hand on the door leading back out to the elevators. The dark haired man had walked back around to the front of the reception desk and was studying him curiously.

"Yes."

"You're Jax's friend," the guy said.

Dane managed a nod.

"Bridget, would you ask Dom to meet me at the diner?"

"Of course, Mr. Bradshaw," she said.

"I'm Logan Bradshaw," the man said as he extended his hand out to Dane.

"Dane Winters."

"Do you have a car, Dane or should we take mine?" Logan asked as he bent down to get a closer look at Emma.

"I have a rental," Dane said in confusion.

"Good. You mind if I drive? Seattle traffic at lunch time can be kind of a mess if you don't know where you're going."

"Where are we going?"

Logan gave Emma a quick tickle before standing. "To see Jax, of course."

~

"*Y*ou okay?" Logan asked as he pulled the car out of the parking garage.

"Yeah," Dane managed to say though Logan's expression said the other man didn't believe him for a second. "How did you know I was Jax's friend?" Dane asked, the term friend sounding completely wrong on his tongue. "Did he tell you about me?" he asked hopefully.

"No, Jax isn't much of a talker. Cade told me about you."

Dane wanted to groan at that. Cade wasn't exactly his biggest fan. He must not have managed to wipe the frown off his face quickly enough at the mention of Cade because Logan laughed and said, "Yeah, Cade has that effect on a lot of people."

Dane sighed. "We didn't exactly hit it off when we met," he admitted.

"Cade can be a little rough around the edges but get him on your side and you've got a friend for life."

Dane fell silent as Logan maneuvered through the crowded streets. As beautiful as the city was, the throngs of people and cars had Dane missing home. But he would give it up in a heartbeat if it meant he could have the life he wanted with Jax.

"Everything will work out, Dane. Have faith," Logan said gently.

Tears stung Dane's eyes. "I think I'm too late," he admitted. "All he asked of me was not to break his heart and that's exactly what I did. Maybe it's not fair to ask for a second chance."

Logan laughed softly. "Never be afraid to ask for a second chance. Dom had to give me a lot of chances before I finally got it right." Logan pulled the car to a stop in front of a newer looking building with at least a dozen floors. "Parking's kind of a pain around here so why don't you head up while I look for a spot? It's 7B."

Dane swallowed back his fear and nodded. He got Emma out of her car seat and headed inside. The elevator to the seventh floor took only seconds and then he was standing in front of Jax's door. He began to shake as he realized his entire life was about to change and he forced himself to knock on the door before he chickened out. But when he saw the man standing on the other side of the door as it opened, his stomach bottomed out and agony tore through him.

"Dane," Cade said in surprise as he finished buttoning up his shirt.

He was too late. Dane felt his knees give out and he managed to lock them just before he crumpled to the floor.

"Jax is in the shower," Cade said. "Come on in. He should be out in a second."

"Uh, no, that's okay. I made a mistake," he managed to get out. "I'm sorry," he mumbled as he turned to leave.

"Dane, wait," he heard Cade call but he was already moving towards the elevator. How had he let this happen? Jax was his. Jax had chosen him.

Dane stopped in his tracks. Jax *was* his. Jax loved *him*. Jax wanted *him*. Dane swung back around and nearly slammed into Cade.

"Dane, listen," Cade began but Dane brushed past him and stalked into Jax's apartment. As soon as Cade entered behind him Dane went on the attack.

"He's mine, Cade. I don't give a shit what you think of me, but he's mine until he tells me he isn't. I don't care how long you've known him – you had your chance."

"Dane-" Cade interjected, his hands out in supplication.

"I may not be some hot, gun-toting, save the world badass like you but I'm a good man. I'm a good father and a loyal friend and I take care of the people I love. I deserve him and he deserves me. So go ahead, try to run me off again and see what happens. Because I love him and I am not leaving until he tells me to go."

"Cade."

Dane turned around to see Jax standing in a doorway behind him and heat flooded his system at the sight of the man who'd changed everything he'd ever known about himself. Seeing Jax with wet hair and wearing just a pair of jeans was a harsh reminder of what he'd walked in on but he shoved it away because it didn't matter.

"Jax, he thinks-" Cade started to say but Jax just shook his head, his dark gaze never leaving Dane's.

God, how had it taken him this long to realize how much he loved this man? Why had he let the voices from his past hold more sway over his decisions than his own heart?

"Hey guys," he heard Logan say from somewhere behind him but he was too lost in Jax's gaze to care at the moment. "Everything okay?" the man asked warily.

Dane's heart lurched against his chest as Jax closed the distance between them. He finally took his eyes off of Dane long enough to focus on Emma and the second he held out his hands, Dane handed her over.

"Hi baby girl," he said softly as he kissed her check and let her grab his face. He held her against his chest as he stepped past Dane.

"You mind watching her for a bit?" he asked Logan.

"Sure, no problem. We'll be at the diner," Logan said.

Dane turned around to see Jax handing Emma to Cade who shook his head. "Jesus, Jax, give her to Logan."

"She knows you," Jax said coolly and gave Cade no choice but to take her. The guy acted like he was being handed a bomb.

"You okay with this?" Logan asked Dane and Dane didn't even hesitate to answer.

"Yes. Her diaper bag is in the back seat of the car."

"Okay, we'll see you guys in a bit," Logan said as he herded Cade out the door.

Jax closed the door and then locked it and a surge of energy went through Dane. Jax was quiet – too quiet. But he also hadn't told him to get the hell out yet.

"You're okay with me sending your daughter off with virtual strangers?"

Jax's cool tone had him on edge but he managed to respond. "You trust them. I trust you."

"So now you trust me? Just like that?"

Dane couldn't blame Jax for not believing him. "No, not 'just like that.' It took longer than it should have but I see it now. You would never hurt me like the others did. Like my parents did."

Jax moved slowly towards him, his dark eyes studying him. "And what about what happened between me and Cade?"

Dane dropped his eyes. "I hate it," he admitted. "But it doesn't change anything."

He felt Jax's fingers under his chin and then his head was being tipped up so he was forced to look into Jax's eyes. "And if I told you nothing happened?"

"I would believe you."

Jax's fingers caressed his skin and Dane shuddered at the need that shot through him.

"I asked you if you loved me and you said no," Jax whispered in a pained voice. "You lied to me."

God, this was torture. The torment he had put this man through...

"I'm so sorry, Jax," he said, a sob catching in his throat. A tear managed to slip down his cheek and he felt Jax's thumb swipe across his skin to wipe it away.

"Just don't do it again," Jax said softly right before he covered Dane's mouth with his.

~

*J*ax felt the tension in his body melt away as Dane let out a little cry and then wrapped his arms around him and returned his kiss.

He'd just stepped out of the shower when he heard the knocking at the front door and then a couple minutes later he'd felt a rush of joy followed by a sharp jab of pain at the sound of Dane's voice. He'd managed to get his pants on and was preparing to go into the living room and send Dane away when he'd heard Dane doing exactly what he'd wanted him to do so long ago – he was fighting for him. For them.

But his wounds ran deep and even Dane's admission of love couldn't take away the cold sense of betrayal that had continued to course through him. As much as he had wanted what Dane was offering, he hadn't been sure he could put his faith in someone that would never be able to do the same. Until Dane had uttered those words that Jax had needed to hear. Dane trusted him. He'd seen the trust in Dane's eyes and he'd known in that instant that he could have the life he wanted and the revelation had nearly brought him to his knees.

Jax forced himself to pull back from Dane and held his face as he said, "Nothing happened between me and Cade. He came over this morning to work out and he used the shower in my guest room to get cleaned up so we could go meet the guys for lunch." He saw the relief go through Dane and he also saw that the man believed him exactly as he'd said he would.

"I love you, Jax. I want to make a life with you. Whether it's here or in Montana or wherever you want to go, I don't care." He pulled Jax down for a brief kiss. "I can't promise that I won't have my little moments where I get scared or say the wrong thing-"

"I'll bring you back, Dane," Jax promised as he wrapped his arms around Dane. "Whenever the noise in your head gets too loud, I'll bring you back."

Jax kissed Dane as he began backing him towards his room. By the time they reached his bed, he'd gotten Dane's shirt off and Dane was struggling to get the button on Jax's jeans free. "Missed you so much," Dane whispered against his lips. Dane's tongue stroked into his mouth and dueled with his while Dane's fingers finished loosening his jeans. Rough palms caressed the globes of his ass as Dane scorched a trail of kisses down his neck and along his collar bone. And then Dane was sliding to his knees as his hands pushed Jax's jeans and underwear down.

Between Dane's expert fingers and hot mouth, Jax was shaking with desire long before Dane sucked him into his mouth and he tangled his fingers into Dane's dark hair and gently fucked into the lushness that was drowning him in liquid fire. Dane's eyes lifted to meet his as he opened his jaw wider and angled his head so Jax could get further down his throat. The open love he saw staring back at him was too much and he reached down to pull Dane to his feet, meeting his mouth halfway and plunging his tongue inside.

He eased Dane down onto the bed and relished in the feel of the hard body that fit his so perfectly. Dane separated his legs so that Jax fit between them and their cocks brushed against each other. Jax reached into his nightstand and pulled out the lube. But when he went to grab a condom, Dane reached for his hand and said, "I want to feel you, Jax. All of you."

Jax was too overwhelmed to speak so he nodded and reached for the lube. His eyes stayed on Dane as he searched out Dane's opening and brushed the tip of his finger over it. Dane bit his lip as he did it over and over and then moaned when Jax's finger breached him. He took his time working more lube into Dane's tight body, reveling in the sounds his lover made as his body hummed with excitement. As he worked, he leaned down and ran his tongue up the length of Dane's cock.

"Yes," Dane hissed as Jax sucked the tip into his mouth and applied suction even as his tongue traced every ridge. He let another finger slide into Dane and Dane shoved his dick farther into Jax's mouth. A hand closed over his head and held him in place as Dane began fucking into him as Jax sawed his fingers in and out of Dane's rippling body.

"More, Jax, please!" Dane moaned as he sat up, forcing Jax to release his cock. Dane pulled Jax's fingers from his body and grabbed him by the hips as he lifted his ass. A hot hand closed over his cock and guided him into position and then Dane was bearing down on him.

"Dane," he whispered as Dane's body opened up beneath him and he slid in as far as he could go. Dane's inner walls twitched along his sensitive cock before he even began moving and he had to suck in a harsh breath to try and gain control of the need firing under his skin.

But Dane took the decision away from him and began pushing his hips up before lowering them slowly back down. Jax let all his weight press down onto Dane and began meeting each upward motion and within minutes he was pinning Dane's hips with his hands so that he could hammer relentlessly into him over and over.

Jax leaned over Dane and kissed him and then in one swift move he pulled out of him and sat back, drawing Dane with him as he went and turning him so that his back was pressed to Jax's front. He slid his cock back into Dane before he could even utter a protest. He wrapped his arms around Dane's chest and felt fingers intertwine with his as Dane began meeting every upward lunge. Their slick skin lit up as the tension in their bodies increased and Jax forced himself to release one of Dane's hands so he could slide it down to the other man's cock. He began stroking Dane mercilessly as his hips punched into Dane over and over.

Dane reached around with one arm and dragged Jax's mouth to his for a searing kiss. "I love you, Jax," Dane whispered against his mouth. "Always."

Jax felt tears prick his eyes as he kissed Dane back. "I love you so much, Dane." He eased Dane forward until he was flat on his stomach, Jax's hand pressed between them on the bed, his fingers still stroking

Dane's shaft. Jax humped into Dane relentlessly, his strokes becoming shorter and shorter as his cock began to pulse and throb in warning. He pressed his head down against the back of Dane's neck as he felt his body draw tighter and tighter.

"It's too much," he whispered against Dane's skin as the tension became nearly unbearable.

He felt Dane's fingers twine around his on the bed. "It'll never be too much, Jax."

Jax slammed into Dane hard and hung there as his release claimed him. Dane cried out as Jax felt his semen bathe Dane's rippling walls and then Dane's cock pulsed in his hand and hot liquid pooled over his fingers. His body continued to convulse uncontrollably as Dane's body throbbed around him, draining everything he had left. As his body began to relax and the pleasure seeped under his skin and along his nerve endings, Jax began to pull out of Dane but the other man reached behind him and grabbed his ass. "Not yet," he said softly as he pressed Jax back into his body.

Jax let his weight sink down onto Dane and he kissed along his neck and shoulders until he reached Dane's waiting lips. He kissed Dane languidly before finally forcing himself to pull out of Dane's body. He shifted off of him long enough to let Dane roll over and then he was on top of him again, his tongue licking over every part of Dane's pliant mouth. He laced their hands together next to Dane's head and noticed Dane's wedding band was gone. Another sign that Dane was truly his now.

It could have been minutes or hours before he finally released Dane and leaned back to study him.

"You stayed in Dare even after I hurt you," Dane said quietly as he ran his fingers through Jax's hair.

"I needed to make sure you were safe."

"Did you know it was Belinda?" Dane asked.

Jax shook his head. "Cade didn't only come out to Montana because he was worried about me. He came because our tech people discovered that someone did hack your phone so they could track your location. Something like that takes sophistication and money. I figured it wasn't about you being gay but I didn't make the connection to Isaac's mother."

"Were you watching me the whole time?"

Jax crossed his arms over Dane's chest and laid his head on them, content to have Dane keep stroking his hair and brushing over his skin with gentle caresses. "Whenever you left the ranch," he admitted.

"Did Rhys know?"

Jax nodded.

"Was Cade there too?"

"No, I sent him home. He was trying to figure out where the hack came from."

Dane fell silent for a moment before saying, "I don't want to come between you and your friend."

"You won't, Dane. Cade knows he messed up. He was trying to protect me." He felt Dane tense beneath him and he suspected the cause. "There's nothing between Cade and me. Never has been. He had no family when Ben and I met him so he just became a part of ours. He knew I was struggling with what was happening with us and he did what he always does – he tried to fix it."

He was glad when Dane relaxed beneath him once again. "Truth is, he feels like shit for the things he said to you and I think you're going to be able to milk this for years to come."

Dane laughed but then sobered. "I know your job means a lot to you – and your friends. I could probably find a practice here in Seattle …"

Jax interrupted him with a kiss. "This place was never home for me. It was a placeholder until I found where I belonged. I want Emma to have the things you wanted for her when you chose Dare. That's home now."

"But your work…"

"Sheriff Granger offered me a job."

"He did?" Dane asked in surprise.

"It was before…" Jax said, reluctant to bring up the day that had torn them apart. "He needs a couple of deputies. He asked Rhys too." Dane went still beneath him and Jax knew he was thinking about the danger he would still face as a law enforcement officer, even in a small town like Dare.

"Would that be enough for you?" Dane asked.

"Anything that means I get to be with you and Emma is enough for me," he said honestly. "I spent years watching humanity at its worst. If all I do for the rest of my life is give out tickets for jaywalking, I'll be a happy man. As long as I can come home to you and Emma at the end of each day."

He saw Dane's eyes shimmer brightly and then he was being pushed onto his back. "I love you, Jaxon Reid."

"I love you, Dane Winters" Jax said with a smile and reached up to run his fingers over Dane's lips. "Let's go get your daughter and go home."

Dane studied him for a long, quiet moment before he kissed Jax softly and said, "Our daughter."

The End

ABOUT THE AUTHOR

Dear Reader,

I hope you enjoyed Dane and Jax's story. They'll be back in Gray and Luke's story.

As an independent author, I am always grateful for feedback so if you have the time and desire, please leave a review, good or bad, so I can continue to find out what my readers like and don't like. You can also send me feedback via email at sloane@sloanekennedy.com

Join my Facebook Fan Group: Sloane's Secret Sinners

Connect with me:
www.sloanekennedy.com
sloane@sloanekennedy.com

ALSO BY SLOANE KENNEDY

(Note: Not all titles will be available on all retail sites)

The Escort Series

Gabriel's Rule (M/F)

Shane's Fall (M/F)

Logan's Need (M/M)

Barretti Security Series

Loving Vin (M/F)

Redeeming Rafe (M/M)

Saving Ren (M/M/M)

Freeing Zane (M/M)

Finding Series

Finding Home (M/M/M)

Finding Trust (M/M)

Finding Peace (M/M)

Finding Forgiveness (M/M)

Finding Hope (M/M/M)

The Protectors

Absolution (M/M/M)

Salvation (M/M)

Retribution (M/M)

Forsaken (M/M)

Vengeance (M/M/M)

A Protectors Family Christmas

Atonement (M/M)

Revelation (M/M)

Redemption (M/M)

Non-Series

Letting Go (M/F)

15438513R00084

Printed in Germany
by Amazon
Distribution